THE AFFAIR OF
THE DEVIANT BISHOP

PAUL FERRAR

**To find out more about this book,
or to contact the author, please visit:
www.vividpublishing.com.au / theaffair**

Copyright © 2024 Paul Ferrar

ISBN: 978-1-923078-20-8
Published by Vivid Publishing
A division of Fontaine Publishing Group
P.O. Box 948, Fremantle
Western Australia 6959
www.vividpublishing.com.au

 A catalogue record for this
book is available from the
National Library of Australia

For Pammy

who travelled these roads with me

This book was written on Ngunnawal land
and the author acknowledges its people as the
traditional owners of the land

A NOTE ON SOME NAMES IN KENYA

This story takes place in 1985. Amboseli and Masai Mara were both called Game Reserves at that time, and I have used those names here. Amboseli is now Amboseli National Park, and Masai Mara is Masai Mara National Reserve.

The name of the local people was at the time spelled Masai, but is now normally spelled Maasai. The National Reserve is sometimes also spelled Maasai Mara now, but in both cases I have used the spelling Masai because it was the one prevalent in 1985.

The Kingdom of Swaziland is now the Kingdom of Eswatini, but it was Swaziland at the time of this story so I have used that name.

A NOTE ON AFRIKAANS WORDS

(the story is set at a time when South Africa had an Afrikaner government)

In Afrikaans the letter 'g' is pronounced like the guttural 'ch' in German. Thus 'Ag' in Afrikaans is pronounced like the German 'Ach'.

'Sies' is an exclamation of annoyance, like 'bah' or 'pah'. It's usually a bit stronger than those, however.

'Man' in exclamations has no gender connotation. It just means 'person' of either gender, rather like 'man' in some modern English (especially American) usage.

Thus 'Ag *sies* man!' as an exclamation means something like 'Oh blast it, man', or even 'Oh shit, man!'.

FIGURE 1: CENTRAL & SOUTHERN AFRICA

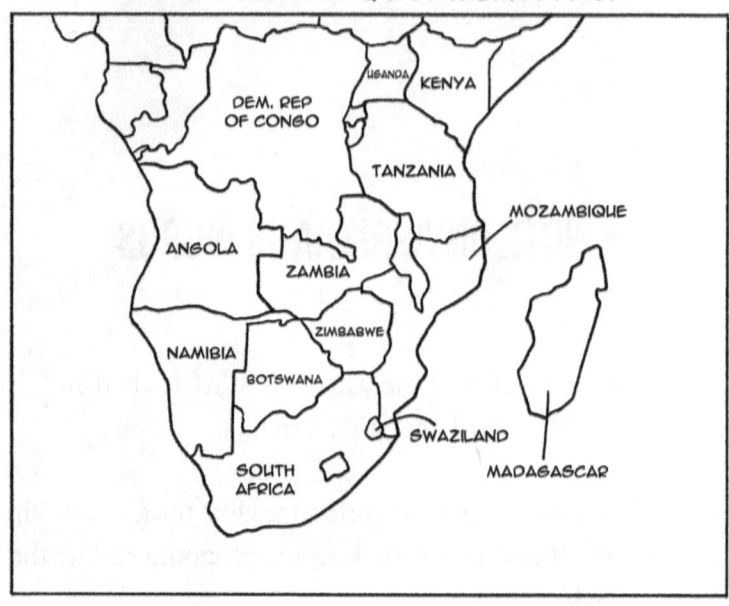

FIGURE 2: KENYA & TANZANIA

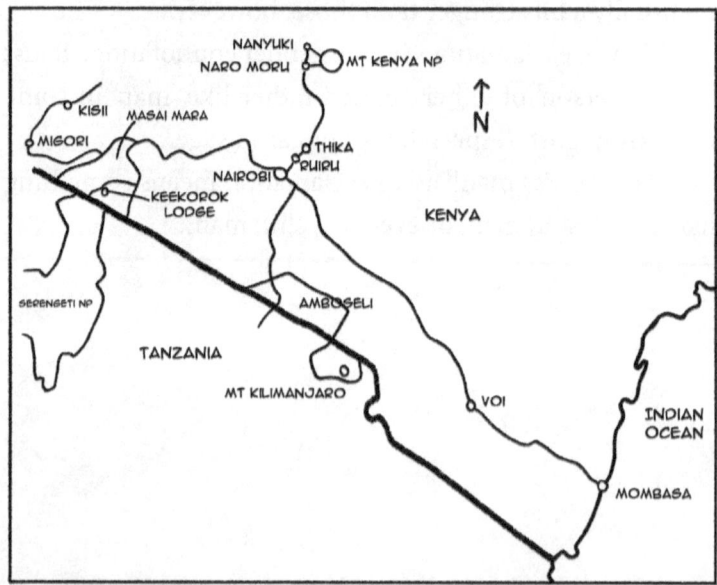

FIGURE 3: BOTSWANA

FIGURE 4: SWAZILAND

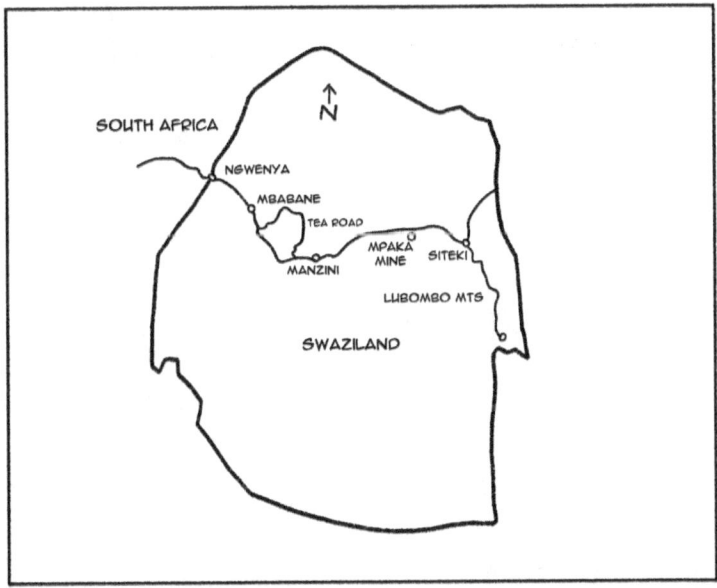

FIGURE 5: SOUTH AFRICA

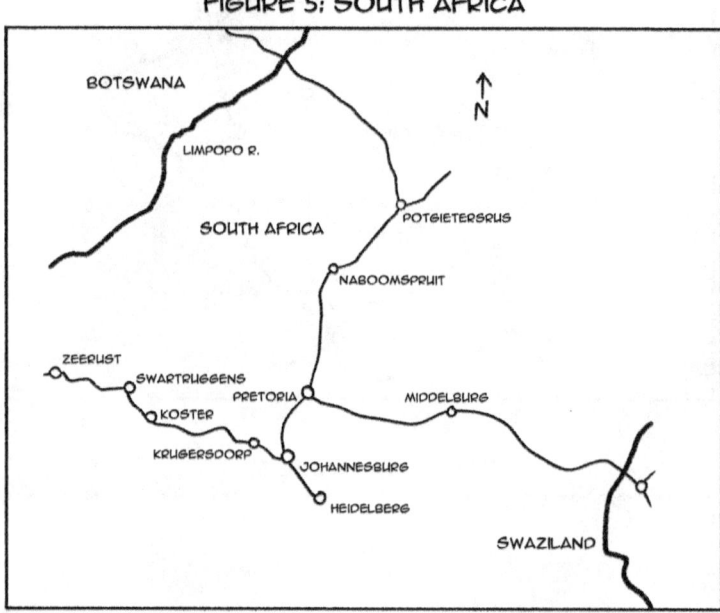

PROLOGUE

EDITORIAL OFFICE OF *THE SUNDAY NEWS*
27 April 1985

The *Sunday News* was jubilant. They were a quality Sunday paper, and the Lord didn't often favour them with stories as good as this one. The news had broken too late for the Saturday papers; the only problem was how to do it with a bit of taste, when the story cried out for sensation.

The *News of the World* would come up with something like:

'AFRICAN TOURIST IN HORROR STABBING, EATING!'

'MAN TORN APART IN MASAI MASSACRE!'

Stuff like that.

'How about 'SPIRALS DOWN TO DEATH'?' suggested someone, thinking of the vultures.

'It'd get all the parachute clubs reading it.' said another.

But the editor said: 'No, we'll just go for TOURIST SPEARED AND EATEN IN AFRICAN GAME PARK.

There won't be a bugger out there who won't be reading that to see what it's all about….'

* * *

Buggers, and others who bought the paper, had Frances Walton to thank for their information. It was her keen eyesight in the Masai Mara Game Reserve in Kenya that led the safari coach to the scene. The vultures were a long way away, but she'd picked them up with her binoculars and pointed them out to the tour leader. He'd been getting increasingly desperate to find a lion for the party. He'd ordered the bus driver from one usually reliable spot to another, but no lions that day. The gods were against him. Must be punishment for what he did to that woman last night...

Maybe this white lady would be his salvation. A plume of vultures was descending – so graceful in flight compared to their clumsiness on the ground, and dropping fast which meant food.

When the bus finally reached the spot there didn't seem to be any lions, though it was hard to see with the long grass. Vultures strode back and forth and bickered; then somebody saw the head of a hyena rise and snap its powerful and bloody jaws at the vultures.

There was great jubilation in the bus, and everyone rushed to the one side to take photographs. Mostly of the long grass. The vultures and the hyena continued to duel intermittently and noisily, but the kill must have been a small one because it was quite hidden in the grass.

They watched for some time while the driver smoked a surreptitious cigarette, and Frances was puzzled by what seemed to be a wooden marker post with a metal end, standing upwards from the kill. Then the hyena gave an extra big heave, and there rose briefly into view something that looked remarkably like a human arm.

'Jesus Christ!' exclaimed one of the watchers, but the others didn't seem to consider this likely and there was un-characteristic silence.

The hyena continued to feed and snap, then eventually gave another big heave and came up with a mouthful of shredded material that looked horribly like clothing. Excited confusion broke out in the bus, not unlike that of the vultures, and the tour leader had to battle to regain control.

He picked Frances and a middle-aged man, who had already shown themselves to be the only level-headed members of the party, and sent them on to the roof of the bus to unpack some tent poles. Then, armed with one of these, he advanced towards the hyena.

The hyena looked up, took a pace backwards and snarled. The tour leader edged close enough to see that there defi-nitely was a man's body, skewered to the ground by what he had recognised as a Masai spear. He summoned the two from the roof with more poles, then shouted to the driver.

'Ibrahim! Take the party and the bus back to the rest camp, and tell the rangers there's a dead man out here. And tell them they'll need to call the police from Nairobi!'

He wasn't going to have his livelihood as a guide ruined by this little problem. The Masai and the government were always fighting over the use of the reserve, and if the Masai had been spearing visitors it would need a senior policeman to handle the matter with a bit of tact. Not the galumphing locals. He would need a bit of tact with his boss at the coach company, too. They wouldn't exactly be happy about this sort of publicity.

Bit odd, too, about the Masai doing this. A bit calculated for their normal style. Who knows, though? Everything's changing these days. Not for the better, either.

The trio managed to drive the hyena back from the body, and after a while it slunk away in disgust. The vultures, now joined by further compatriots and two sinister-looking marabou storks, were not so easily deterred, and the party had had plenty of exercise with the poles by the time the rangers arrived, followed some time later by some very senior police.

At that point the story ran thin on fact, and big on horror-struck reminiscence and anecdotes from members of the bus party. In particular from those who had had the least to do with the matter.

The only other notable fact was that the victim was as yet unidentified. He had been wearing a nondescript light shirt, shorts and sandals, and there were no papers on him. And part of his face had been eaten away by the hyena, so that all the police would say was that he was a European.

NICHOLAS TWISTLETON

_1_

I don't know what it is, but some days just don't start right. I got up an hour earlier than I meant to because I misread the clock. Then we were out of proper coffee and I had to use instant. Then the electric kettle burned out and I had to dig out our old camping cooker. At least it had enough gas left in it to boil a saucepan.

And then there was the depressing story in the Sunday papers about the African tourist being killed. Depressing because I'd much rather have been in Africa than here in England. Depressing because life must be changing over there and I'm obviously losing touch. When Marion and I lived there, the Masai wouldn't have killed someone in cold blood like they had according to the paper. They were quite ready to jab a spear at you or chuck a knobkerrie if you tried to photograph them without permission – meaning without a fee – but that was the hot-blooded response of a warrior who'd been insulted. This sounded a bit more deliberate.

Must be watching too much television.

I was pondering all this when the front door shot open,

then slammed loudly. Anyone who didn't know might have thought that a fireball or a small tornado had entered the room. It circled several times and came to rest on the lounge.

'Hi Nico' it said.

'Hi Marion. Welcome back! How are you? Survive the students this year?'

'Some coffee'd be good, thanks.'

'Only instant, I'm afraid. And I'll have to boil it on the primus because the kettle seems to have burnt out.'

'Christ, you're useless. Two weeks away and the place has fallen to pieces.'

A bit unfair because both had only just happened, and it must have been Marion who used the last of the real coffee. But things like that always happen when I'm with Marion. Bad luck doesn't happen to her. It wouldn't dare.

I made the coffee, which she sniffed twice and glared at, but it seemed to go down all right.

'It was quite a good field course this year, actually, apart from a bit much rain. We had two really bright students. No major troublemakers, which was a nice change after last year. Three of the girls are likely to be pregnant if they weren't taking precautions, and there'll probably be a couple of good scientific papers out of the fortnight.'

'Sounds about normal. What'll the papers be on?'

'Well, the really good one'll be on a freshwater leech as the intermediate host of a duck parasite. At least it looks as though that's what happens – we've set up an infection trial and we've just got to wait for the parasite to develop to confirm it. I've got the duck in the car, actually – we'll have to keep it here for a couple of weeks to let the parasite hatch and develop to the stage where we can identify it.'

Things like that were always happening. Our home was host to all sorts of fauna, though a diseased one was new.

'This parasite going to infect us too?'

'No, it does disgusting things to the duck but it doesn't attack humans. Unless I've got the identification wrong.'

A comfort, that.

'Well, it'll give you something to talk about at the next College dinner. If you sit next to Professor Lazenby, you could probably get her to throw up. She nearly did at the last feast when you were going on about how vultures tear carrion apart.'

'Better than her rabbiting on about the minutiae of Etruscan civilisations. Anyway, what have you been doing apart from destroying the place?'

'Not much, really. The destruction took time. On a different subject, read this.'

I gave her the Sunday papers, which had the African murder blazed all over the front pages.

As she read – intently, frowning and fast, which was typical – I wondered once again how Marion and I had come together, and why she'd stayed. I tend to be a bit slow and deliberate about things, and normally Marion can't stand slow people. We also made a bit of an odd pair, with me tall and gangling, and she – well, I think dumpy is the technical expression, though certainly not to her face.

It was actually in Masai Mara that we met. I was working in Amboseli Masai Game Reserve at first, but sometimes travelled to the Mara for extra studies. Marion had been in Mara, doing a PhD through Oxford University on the ecology of the Martial Eagle. She's a small person physically, but nothing else is on a small scale where Marion is concerned. She had to study just about the largest bird of prey in Africa. Come to think of it, only Marion would have been a match for such a fierce bird, though even she came off second best in some of their encounters.

I was doing a PhD through a rather lesser university, on African penduline tits – elegant little birds whose main claim to fame was that they weave fine and elegant, pear-shaped nests that hang from branches by a woven stalk. The nests even have a false entrance and chamber to fool predators – the real entrance is cleverly concealed. Much more subtle than large and fierce predators, but any such comment doesn't go down well with Marion.

A naturalist had claimed in the past that my small birds were sometimes prey for Martial eagles, but that was quickly disproved. The eagles thought much bigger than that – nothing smaller than game birds, and preferably things like ground squirrels, hares, rodents, monkeys and snakes. So there was no association between our projects, but by the time my project finished we'd drifted into a sort of unspoken association ourselves. Definitely an attraction of opposites.

We worked together at Mara for a while, and then both our grants ran out and we had to return to the UK. Marion's assumption seemed to be that we would stay living together, which was fine by me. It was a situation full of creative tension, but it seemed to work.

Most of the time.

Sort of.

At least Marion hadn't made jokes about the penduline tits, unlike most of my male colleagues. Even my Vice Chancellor was forever asking me if I'd seen any droopy African tits lately. It wasn't particularly funny the first time. Marion would never make fun of such things. The male anatomy maybe, but not tits. She gets pretty fierce on jokes with birds as a double meaning. You don't mess with women or birds when Marion's around.

'Doesn't sound like the Masai's usual sort of stunt. What's going on over there these days?'

'Dunno. Didn't quite ring true to me, either, but I guess we're losing touch. They must be watching too many movies or something.' And we didn't think about it any further.

Until a couple of weeks later, that is.

_ 2 _

Meanwhile, in the Amboseli Game Reserve, another killing had just been carried out. The victim was tall and grey, and he had been followed by four black men for the previous day and a half. The men were not Masai but Somalis, renowned for their tracking ability.

Their orders had come from a white man, although they had never seen him. A black intermediary had told them the location of the target, and had driven them to a spot nearby. From there they had made their way with stealth and speed, picking up likely tracks and soon finding the target, who was browsing on an acacia. They carefully took out arrows, the heads sharp and tipped with poison, and two of them fired towards some of the softer folds of the tough and wrinkled hide. As he felt the jabs, the elephant snorted slightly and raised his head, displaying his magnificent tusks. He hesitated for a moment, then decided the spot was uncomfortable and wandered off. All his pursuers had to do was follow.

They walked for a considerable distance. The elephant became at first irritable, then uncertain. He began to lurch and stagger, and his track became crooked and confused. After a little more than a day he fell over.

He managed to regain his feet, but not for much longer.

The men did not approach too closely for a while. From experience they knew how much a fallen elephant could still move, and how far it could lash with its trunk. They watched for tell-tale signs of muscular collapse.

One man moved cautiously forward and poked at the elephant's trunk with a stick. The trunk convulsed a little, but did not otherwise move. He signalled, and the others moved quickly forward with knives and an axe. They sliced into the skin and flesh of the elephant where the tusk was inserted, exposing its root until they could hack it out, dragging it away from the mass of soft tissue that ran up its core. The elephant continued to breathe and the trunk continued to twitch, but the poor beast could do nothing to stop them.

The underneath tusk was more difficult, but one man, hot and bloody, lay half under the elephant's head and slashed away hide and meat until the other three could drag out the tusk. They wrapped the tusks in cloth covers that they carried, and made their way quickly from the scene.

Two men carried one tusk, each of which weighed about 35 kilos. They crossed the rather open ground as fast as possible, senses alert for approaching tours or safari parties, which they would be able to detect well before they themselves were seen. They made for relatively wooded country where they would be covered from the air, the only direction from which they were at all vulnerable. They paused only at a waterhole to drink, and to wash off blood, sweat and dust. Too much blood could have aroused comment.

As far as possible they stuck to trees, and timed themselves to arrive at a particular group of thorn trees about an hour before sunset. The truck was there, as it had been at the same time the day before, and would have been on subsequent days until the men arrived. Nobody could forecast how far the Somalis would have had to travel before they were able to get the tusks.

The driver of the truck stood in silence. He was also black, but with features very different from the four hunters – broader, flatter and blacker than the elongate and fine brown faces of the Somalis. He watched them stow the two bundles in the truck, then handed each some money and they vanished. Not a word was said throughout. The driver threw some other covers roughly over the packages so that they looked like a scattered heap of tarpaulins, raised the tailgate and drove off. And the tusks began their circuitous journey towards the remaining ivory markets of the world.

_ 3 _

I didn't hear what she said at first, because she was in the lounge room and I was in the kitchen glugging wine. Not imbibing, you understand, but making glugging sounds pouring it over a duck.

And before you jump to any conclusions, no, it wasn't Marion's parasitised duck. That was still looking fit and healthy. It was crapping all over the back garden, and was eating plants that I was quite fond of. This duck was dead and trussed, and the wine was an optimistic attempt to make it more palatable than the previous ones.

Some months ago I'd been given a small grant by a conservation group to study seasonal changes in the diet of wild ducks. I think they're hoping to use the results to get a ban on a new housing area that's being planned. It's a hot local issue, and the greenies are prepared to sacrifice a few ducks in the greater cause of defeating the local builders, conspicuous among whom is the local Mayor.

So my assistant has a permit to catch and kill two ducks a month through the year, and we cut them open to read the entrails. We haven't foretold anything of great interest from the guts, but then we're only amateurs compared to the Sibyls. We haven't found much of interest inside the intestines either – mostly lots of grass, and a few snails – so I don't think the conservationists are going to be too excited either. But it'll be too late by the time they find out. Maybe I'll have to embellish the report a bit, because I'm not keen on the housing development either.

I hate waste, and I don't like to discard the rest of the bird after its guts have contributed to science, so my assistant and I alternate with one for the pot. The variety of recipes for wild duck is not enormous and the appeal's wearing a bit thin now. The assistant's last duck went to his cat, which he said wasn't too impressed either.

Anyway, I thought I heard Marion swearing loudly, which isn't all that common but neither is it unknown. I thought maybe she'd discovered yet another deficiency in my activities, so I just kept glugging. However, she appeared almost immediately at the kitchen hatch.

'Bloody hell, Nico – look at this!' She waved a newspaper at me, narrowly avoiding marinating it along with the duck.

Where her finger pointed I read a small news paragraph:

DEAD TOURIST IDENTIFIED

Nairobi Police have released the name of the man speared to death and partially eaten by a hyena in a Kenya game reserve two weeks ago. He was Mr Fergus Campbell, a retired white police officer who had been living in Mombasa. No arrests have yet been made.

For a moment Marion said nothing, which was also uncharacteristic.

Then she said: 'It's ridiculous! Fergus wouldn't have got himself speared by the Masai, not under any circumstances. He practically lived among them, for God's sake. He was a blood brother, almost. Even young hotheads would have known that. I simply don't believe it!'

I couldn't add anything to that analysis, so I didn't.

* * *

That night in bed I couldn't sleep. I felt deeply sad that a genuinely good bloke like Fergus Campbell had died. He was one of the best of police officers, like the old colonial style – gentle in manner but ruthless in the pursuit of crime and corruption. He had a soft Scottish accent, and the humour and determination of a true Scot. He treated everyone fairly, but when they proved themselves unworthy of fairness he went after them mercilessly.

Perhaps unusually for a policeman, he was also kind in quiet and unsung ways to people who deserved it, and he had quite a few among the general population who'd also have grieved for his passing. Fewer in the police, however – his pursuit of corruption certainly didn't go down well with all. That also accounted for the fact that he never rose above Inspector, even though his skills could have taken him much higher. He said it didn't worry him because it gave him the freedom to fight crime instead of to administer, but

I'd always thought that it must have rankled a bit.

Fergus was very kind to us when we were in Kenya. We met him quite early on, when we were trying to set up a tent in the main campground of Masai Mara and were having trouble. He happened to be passing, and after observing us for a few moments he came over and said:

'It doesn't seem to be going too well, does it? I take it you haven't used this particular equipment much before?'

Which was kinder than saying "You look like a right pair of amateurs, don't you?".

He helped us get the tent up and pegged, then asked us what we were doing in the park. When we told him about our bird studies there he became quite interested, and we realised later that he was quite a good field naturalist. He had an even greater knowledge of the Masai, and clearly admiration and an affection for them and their way of life. His family had done it tough in a croft in Scotland, and I guess he respected others who could live well under hard and primitive conditions.

A little later he introduced us to some key figures in the Masai community and told them about our work, and that was a great help to us as we struggled to learn in some depth about the birds of Kenya. The Masai almost certainly knew more about the birds than we would ever find out with our research, and I often wondered whether they were scornful about our rather amateurish attempts. If so, they were too polite to show it.

The other thing that was niggling in my mind was the

story that Fergus was retired, with the implication that he was just in Masai Mara as a tourist. Just before we left he'd said that he was being put on to a special assignment, but he didn't say what it was. He was certainly nowhere near retirement age, and unless he'd been deliberately pushed out of the force by those who didn't like him, he would have still been working when he died. It was so annoying that he didn't tell us what it was, but maybe he couldn't afford to tell anyone.

I eventually drifted into sleep, and dreamed that I was back in the African bush with shapeless and unidentified predators stalking after me.

* * *

Next day Marion had evidently been thinking about Fergus as well.

'That stuff in the paper about Fergus – it has to be a load of rubbish,' she said. 'The bit about him being a tourist or something in Masai Mara can't be right. He always went to Scotland when he went on leave – you know that. He spent half his life in Masai reserves. Why on earth would he holiday there?'

'I was thinking exactly the same last night too. I also think it was bullshit about him being retired, and I recalled something he said just before we left. D'you remember he was muttering about being transferred to a special project? I wonder if this had something to do with that?'

We looked at each other in silence for a moment.

'So?' said Marion.

'So?'

'A MacTaggart owes it to a Campbell to do something....'

Marion had made much while in Kenya of her family having fought on the same side of the glen as the Campbells. Whichever glen that was – I was never sure. But I'd had a lot of time for Fergus and I felt we owed him something too. He didn't have anybody out there who would have looked after his interests.

'Go to Kenya, you mean?'

'It would be nice, wouldn't it...? I mean we could ask a few questions about what was going on....'

She wasn't game to ask the most pertinent question, but she was willing me to answer it with a stare that would have done Franz Mesmer credit. I bit the bullet.

'It would be a suitable outlay for the Trust, if that's what you're thinking.'

Bingo.

It wasn't really a trust, but that's what we called it to each other. Marion and I have spent most of our existence together in a fairly penniless state, academic pay at our level being minimal, but I'm in the lucky state of having a nest-egg to draw on. Though I would have preferred not to have it, because my father died to provide it.

My mother had died quite soon after I was born, but my father survived until I was just about adult. I don't think he quite knew what to do with an only son, but he mainly didn't worry because he had to run a small family brewery which took all his time. He did know what to do with that and the brewery was a great success, which was perhaps why a large national company made Dad an offer that he couldn't refuse. Though he did try quite hard to reject it.

He was never happy again after the brewery went, and he died soon afterwards. I could see the spark simply go out. He left me the proceeds of the sale, but I'd been so sickened and angered by what I'd seen that I didn't want anything to do with it.

I stuck it in a savings account and vowed never to touch it, except for using it to take on unethical behaviour by someone else. I know it sounds corny and a bit like Batman or someone, but it made a lot of sense to me. Most of all I would have liked to use it to sink the brewery that now ran Twistleton's, but they weren't leaving themselves open for many opportunities.

In the meantime, finding out what had happened to Fergus did seem to qualify. And there were a few side benefits too.

'We could eat goat instead of duck,' said Marion wistfully. 'And Mombasa curries...'

'I'm on if you are. I've finished marking, and the last examiners' meeting's on Friday. After that I'm free for three months, nearly.'

'I guess I could manage it too. Murdoch can do the August and September ducks, and I could start writing the first report in Kenya . . . mm, I like it. Shall I go and see the bank in the morning?'

Marion simply grinned.

_4_

KENYA

It wasn't quite the arrival I would have liked, but at least we were back. Flying isn't one of my favourite activities. I'm with Michael Flanders who said that if God had intended us to fly, He would never have given us the railways. It was a bumpy flight for much of the way, including the landing where we seemed to bounce up and down on the runway like a pebble skimming on water. At least that's how my inside registered it.

Still, we were back. And when the plane doors opened and we climbed out into the crisp morning air, the sensations were like a tonic. The smell of tropical vegetation – admittedly mixed with aviation fuel, but it was still there. The different feel of the air in your face, and the gentle humidity. Birds were singing a dawn chorus as we walked towards the terminal building, and the hibiscus hedge along the walkway had the luxuriant blooms that you only get in the tropics.

My heart skipped a little as I knew we were back, and

even Marion looked slightly excited.

Inside the terminal there were even more black faces than at Heathrow. The passport, customs and currency checks seemed to be going in slow motion, but at least they went and we had no problems.

We'd declared ourselves as tourists on our immigration cards, though we'd also telexed a couple of departments before we left to say we were coming to finish off an ornithological investigation. Both statements were partly true, and we hoped that both would give us a good excuse for poking round in game parks.

In the arrival hall, a voice came from one of the pillars.

'Twelve cold beers at the Norfolk, then!'

A lean, tanned figure detached itself from the pillar and ambled towards us, sandals slapping against the stone floor. With faded khaki shirt, shorts and battered sunhat, he was the archetypal expatriate figure.

'Hujambo, habari gani?'

'Mzuri tu.'

I didn't think it would come back so easily.

Peter Marston kissed Marion, and shook my hand with surprising warmth.

'You do recall the bet, don't you? Twelve beers if you came back within twelve months, and I make it ten. I marked it on our kitchen calendar in case there was any argument.'

'It's worth the beer and more just to be back,' said Marion. 'And good of you to come and meet us this early. Is Monika with you?'

I could hear the curiosity in her voice, and I was busting to know too. Peter's first wife Ann had died in an accident while we were in Kenya. Soon after we left, Peter sent us a letter to say he'd married someone called Monika – who certainly hadn't been visibly on the scene while we were there. All he'd written was that he'd married for the sake of the children.

'No, Jeff was the only one who was up to the early start. He's around here somewhere...'

At that moment Jeffrey roared past, practising a take-off up the passenger hall. Peter persuaded him to abort the mission, and he taxied out with the rest of us to an incredibly battered Land Rover in the car park.

'You haven't *still* got that old wreck?' said Marion. 'It was in a state of collapse even before we left last year.'

'This is the new one. The old one's back home, with manure in it for the garden.'

Peter covered the dusty seat with an equally dusty blanket for us, stowed Jeffrey and the luggage in the back and roared off, trailing smoke down the airport road.

* * *

The house was in the hills some way out of Nairobi; an old wooden house, white-painted, wide-verandahed. It stood at the end of a frangipani-lined driveway, where the air was refreshingly cool.

It was also very noisy as the Land Rover arrived. The vehicle was enveloped by children the moment it stopped.

Jeffrey was joined by his sister and brothers, and two black children belonging to the servant were just as keen to see the exotic visitors. The servant herself stood in the shade of the verandah, watching shyly and curiously.

Monika had obviously decided to let the reunions happen first. She appeared after the children had had time to get over their first wave of excitement. And when she did appear, I couldn't have had a greater shock.

Ann had been slight, darkly Celtic and very feisty. Monika was startlingly blond and large. With breastplate and helmet, shield and sword, she could have been match or mate for any Norse god, and Wagner would have loved her. But her voice was unexpectedly mild, with a lilting Scandinavian intonation, and I found I'd braced myself unnecessarily when she shook my hand.

A tantalising smell of baking soon became a breakfast of fresh rolls, papaya and lime juice, with fragrant Kenyan coffee. Marion as one of the world's great eaters did full justice to it. I was still feeling wobbly from the flight and was more moderate.

By the end of breakfast I was already feeling part of the family. And remarkably, Monika seemed the centre of the family and the children seemed to be accepting her as though they had known no other mother. She may have looked like a Rhinemaiden but she was actually a very calming sort of person. Even I began to feel I'd known her for years.

We spent the day relaxing, enjoying the life of expatriates in Kenya. We swam in a pool behind the house, we ate, we played with the children, we took them for a walk in the bush; then towards evening we sat and watched familiar birds in the garden. Unnatural death was not obviously on anyone's mind.

* * *

Next morning I consulted with Marion, and she agreed with me there was a risk we could be seduced into tropical sloth and forget why we'd come, so after breakfast we raised the main purpose of the visit with Peter. We'd always thought he was someone you could trust.

'Yes, you mentioned in your letter about Inspector Campbell,' said Peter. 'I never met him, I'm afraid, so I don't know anything about what he might have been doing.'

'What did the papers say about it?'

'Well, it was rather curious really. I've been back through all the old papers, which we had in a pile in the shed, and that's all there was.' He handed a solitary clipping to Marion. 'There was much more in the cuttings you sent me than there is in that.'

There certainly wasn't a problem with lurid headlines or sensational reporting in the Kenyan press. MAN DIES IN MARA was the headline, followed by a couple of flatly factual paragraphs. On page 15.

'Extraordinary,' said Marion. 'It's not as though that sort of incident happens here all the time. Surely they could have made a better story out of it than that?'

'Well, there was a bit of a fuss going on at the time about corruption in the City Council – it was all over the front of the paper that this came out of. But I agree it's odd that they didn't make a more dramatic story out of it. The Post's not normally known to miss a good sensation.'

'It sounds to me as though someone told them to hush up the story,' said Marion.

Silence…

'So where do we go from here?' asked Marion. 'I mean, we can't just bowl into the Police Station and say "Hi, we're investigating the death of one of your men – what can you tell us about it?" But we really need to know what Fergus was doing in the Mara.'

There was another silence.

'Perhaps I could introduce you to Ezekiel,' said Monika, from the background.

Three pairs of eyes turned to look at her.

'Ezekiel is a Police Inspector in Nairobi. I used to be a social worker there, you know. I had quite a lot to do with him at times over certain cases, and I always believed that he was one of the honest ones there. I'll go and call him now.'

She returned a little while later to say: 'He wasn't too keen, but I've persuaded him at least to meet you. It'll be up to you then.'

'That's great!' said Marion. 'I'm sure Nico can convince him that our motives are the purest. Which station is he based at?'

'He doesn't want you anywhere near the Police Station.

He's going to meet us for coffee. At half past ten this morning, actually. I said we'd meet him at the Thorn Tree. I have to go marketing anyway, so I thought it would be a good opportunity.'

'Half past ten? We can't get to Nairobi by then, can we?'

'Oh yes, no problem. But we ought to go in the next ten minutes or so.'

That didn't give us much time to get ready, let alone plan a strategy for our talk to Ezekiel. But we figured we'd be able to do this on the way down to Nairobi.

We'd reckoned without Monika's driving...

* * *

Monika not only looked like a Rhinemaiden, but her style of driving was Ride of the Valkyries. We soon discovered why there would be no problem reaching Nairobi by ten thirty. We roared down the hillsides, the two tyres that remained on the road screeching at each bend, and the vehicle creaking in protest. I decided that maybe air travel wasn't so bad after all, and even Marion looked a bit tense. This must have been Monika's way of making up for her otherwise mild manner.

In the Nairobi traffic it was just as bad, but somehow other vehicles always cleared around us, even if only by a hair's breadth. Probably most of the Nairobi drivers had learned to recognise what was coming.

We fluked a parking space near the market, somewhat to the indignation of another driver who thought he'd fluked it just ahead of us. We set off at a brisk trot for the New Stanley Hotel, and made it by twenty-eight minutes past ten.

Monika couldn't see Ezekiel, but we sat down at a table near the Thorn Tree and ordered coffee for four.

'He'll be here,' said Monika. 'He tends to materialise suddenly.'

The Thorn Tree is an odd relic of more intrepid colonial days. A large thorn tree standing in the open courtyard of the original Stanley Hotel was used by explorers and hunters, who fastened messages for other travellers to its trunk. Such message trees became a bit of a tradition in nineteenth century Africa – one even existed in remote Ngamiland, in the wilds of the Bechuanaland Protectorate near the Kalahari Desert. The Nairobi tree was the most famous, but the original tree eventually rotted away and the current one was a replacement, still in use but boarded around its base to prevent it being ringbarked by drawing pins.

It looked a bit artificial in the urban courtyard of the New Stanley, protected by neat boards and without a lion in sight. There were a lot of messages pinned to the boards, and plenty of tourists intrepidly wandering round peering at them. Even surreptitiously lifting the corners of folded notes to read them. I was finding it quite entertaining watching the antics, and the comings and goings in the courtyard.

However, I missed one of the comings. I was suddenly aware that a tall African was bending over talking to Monika, who was waving him to the fourth chair. I then realised that I'd noticed the man a few minutes before, standing where

Monika wouldn't have been able to see him, probably observing us. But discreetly enough that I hadn't given it any real attention.

Monika introduced us to Ezekiel, who chatted to Monika for a bit about mutual acquaintances in the prostitution business, and what had happened to whom since Monika gave up her social work. When she'd finished her coffee she got up and excused herself to go to the market.

After a pause Marion said a little tentatively: 'Did Monika tell you what we wanted to talk to you about?'

Ezekiel said nothing, but coolly appraised both of us. Suddenly he said: 'What can you tell me about Byron Carpenter?'

The question was so unexpected that it left us both speechless for a moment.

'You are supposed to be experts on birds. What can you tell me about Byron Carpenter?' He repeated the question quite sharply.

Marion collected her wits first.

'He's an American professor. He's curator of the Beagle-hole Museum of Ornithology at Harvard University. He's supposed to be one of the world's best ornithologists.'

'He's also a superb bird photographer,' I added. 'National Geographic regularly features articles and pictures by him.'

'Do you think he could be corrupt or dishonest?'

'I've never met him,' said Marion. 'Have you, Nico?'

I shook my head. 'I guess neither of us could say anything about that. But it would shake ornithology to its core if he was. He's the much-loved father figure of the bird world. It would be a bit like Saint Francis of Assisi being caught smuggling protected wildlife.'

Ezekiel looked at me sharply as I said that.

'Did you have a special reason for using that example?'

I was getting increasingly puzzled, and shook my head.

'Okay,' said Ezekiel. 'What you told me about Byron Carpenter is about the same as the FBI said.'

He allowed himself a faint smile at our reaction, because he knew he was playing with us. He snapped his fingers at a waiter and ordered some more coffee. When this had been served, he leaned towards us and spoke in a voice that wouldn't carry to adjoining tables.

'Okay, I will talk to you. Tell me first what you know about Fergus Campbell.' His rich African voice was quite musical; his English almost flawless, a little more precise than that of a native-born Englishman.

Marion spoke first.

'Fergus was a good friend of ours – both of us. You know we used to work in Amboseli and the Mara?'

Ezekiel nodded. 'I know.' He appeared to have been well-briefed on us.

'We ran into each other often enough that we got to know him – had a few drinks at rest houses, learned a lot about East Africa and the Masai from him, watched birds together sometimes. He was a very good field naturalist, you know?'

Ezekiel nodded again, but said nothing.

'Okay, when we read the account of Fergus's death in the British papers, two things struck us as odd about it. First, it implied that he'd been murdered by Masai, but the description didn't sound like the sort of thing Masai might do. Too premeditated and cold-blooded. And secondly, we both felt we knew Fergus well enough to be sure that he wouldn't have been in the Mara except on work, but the article said he was a retired policeman holidaying there. It just didn't sound right. He said something to us when we left last year about going on to a special project. We wondered whether that had something to do with it?'

'And exactly what were you proposing to do about it?'

Marion looked a little disconcerted, and glanced at me. Thanks, Marion.

'I guess it was partly an excuse to come back to Kenya. But we thought we might ask a few questions on the spot, and if it seemed appropriate poke around a bit. Research biologists are well known for poking about everywhere.' It sounded very lame. 'You probably think that's very naive, however.'

Ezekiel stared at us, or maybe through us. He sighed, and spoke.

'Okay. You are quite right, of course, about the killing. We are sure the Masai had nothing to do with it. Fergus was hit on the back of the head, probably knocked unconscious but not killed. He was then stretched out and the spear was driven through his heart. He was pinned firmly to the ground, and he eventually died from loss of blood. We hope he never recovered consciousness.'

His voice had become harsher.

'It was a Masai spear that killed him, though, wasn't it?'

Ezekiel nodded.

'Well, couldn't you find out who the maker was, and get a lead on who might have bought it? I believe every spear's unique, and the makers tend to remember what happened to each?'

'We thought of that,' replied Ezekiel, possibly with a touch of scorn. 'It was apparently an old spear, and nobody living could tell us anything about it. It might have come from a collection, but nobody recognised it. And it had no fingerprints anywhere on it. Not quite the average Masai killing, was it?'

'So it could have been almost anybody?' said Marion.

'Oh no, we're pretty sure we know who did it,' said Ezekiel.

He was playing with us again, and once more he enjoyed our astonishment.

'Did you ever meet Charles Pendleton while you were here?'

'I heard a bit about him, and I met him once,' I replied. 'I instinctively disliked him. Arrogant, and I wouldn't have trusted him.'

'I remember him distinctly,' said Marion, with feeling. 'He made a pretty determined pass at me in the bar at Keekorok Lodge once.'

This time it was only me showing surprise. That was one

bit of Marion's past I hadn't been aware of.

'The special assignment Fergus Campbell was on was the investigation of ivory poaching in the game parks of Kenya. As you know, this is becoming an increasing problem here. Not helped by the involvement of some greedy politicians.'

His tone as well as his expression showed his disgust.

'We had one message from Fergus to say that he had discovered an organised operation with Charles Pendleton as the ringleader. He was going to try to get some hard evidence that could be used in court. And that was the last we heard from him. We got no evidence at all, because if he did manage to get hold of anything it must have been removed from his tent. We found only his personal effects.'

'Is there any evidence that points towards Pendleton other than Fergus's report?'

'No, but it doesn't seem likely that anyone else would have had a motive. There were no signs of ordinary theft. I suppose Pendleton could have got one of his assistants from the safari camp to do it, but I think he would have made sure and done it himself. He wouldn't have trusted a kaffir – as he would call them – to do it properly, or at least not to give it away afterwards. He has made a point of asking us several times if we have caught the culprit yet. He is laughing up his sleeve at the stupid black bastards, I'm sure of it.'

Something came back to mind. 'Am I right in thinking Pendleton used to hunt game?

'Oh yes. Bwana Pendleton was one of the great white hunters of Kenya at one time.' Ezekiel's lip was curling even more now. 'Then hunting became illegal and he set up the safari company that he runs now. Huntsman Safaris, he had to call it. An arrogant man. He is said to be a very good shot, and we are quite sure he hasn't given up hunting.'

'So he may well have killed Fergus, but there's no evidence to link him to the crime, right?'

'It's worse than that. He has an apparently unshakeable alibi for the period during which the murder must have been committed.'

He fixed us with a penetrating stare.

'He was in Amboseli at the time. Taking Professor Byron Carpenter on an exclusive bird-watching safari...'

* * *

We digested this further blow to our prospects as criminal investigators.

Finally Marion said: 'Well, I guess there isn't much we can do about an alibi like that. But we can still poke around and see if we can get more evidence about Pendleton's poaching operation. Wouldn't that be of some use?'

'It would be of very great help if you could do that. But I must warn you of the danger. Fergus Campbell was an experienced policeman and he was killed. Bwana Pendleton is an experienced hunter, and such men are alert to investigators and danger. And I must emphasise that the police cannot help you. I have not spoken to you today, and I know nothing about your plans. You understand...?'

'We understand. But we'll only be a couple of harmless biologists poking around after birds and animals in the bush.'

'Yes, well, remember that Mr Charles Pendleton is not a harmless animal. If you discover anything that you wish to tell me, here is my card. Just phone me and invite me for coffee at the Thorn Tree. Do not leave any other message at the police station. It is possible that the poachers have bribed some members of the police force.'

He stood up to go. The sense of power and authority was palpable.

'I wish you luck. Fergus was a good friend, and I don't like ivory poachers. Go safely.'

And he went.

'Whew!' said Marion. 'I feel as though I've just been interrogated.'

'I think we just were.'

_ 5 _

The ride back with Monika was a little slower than the descent. There were the fruits and vegetables to consider this time. We discussed the pros and cons of travelling to Masai Mara, and the pros won without much of a fight. It was our main reason for coming to Africa, after all.

Following lunch we got together a scratch lot of camping gear from the Marstons. Peter offered the use of the older Land Rover if we cared to remove the garden manure from it – fortunately this was in plastic bins rather than as delivered by nature, and we gladly accepted. We collected food from Monika, totally failed in our battle to pay for it, dug out maps, phoned the park for a campsite reservation, and finally began to feel we were getting somewhere. Not to mention also sweaty, so we decided to cool off in the pool.

We went to change, and joined the children splashing around in the water. A little while later Monika walked up to the edge of the pool, peeled off all her clothes and plumped in amongst us. I had to work hard not to gape in amazement. I told Marion afterwards that the level of the pool had risen several inches, and she murmured about small hippos, then said that was unfair.

* * *

Next morning we were actually on our way. We drove early out of the hills and into flatter country. It was still morning as we crossed the Loita Plains. A herd of Thomson's gazelle scattered away in front of us, and I felt I was back where I wanted to be.

Secretary birds strode across the grass, kicking at it to disturb small animals. Zebras scuffed up dust. Large herds of Masai cattle meandered along with their cloaked herdsmen, some of whom acknowledged a wave while others stood mutely watching.

Along the road there were Masai warriors in twos and threes – tall, proud figures carrying spears almost as long as themselves, red cloaks wrapped around otherwise naked bodies, heads partly shaved with the remaining hair plaited and rubbed with grease and pigment.

Parking the Land Rover at the Masai Mara reserve entrance, Marion battled her way through the souvenir sellers. They swooped on the white target like a flock of vultures, until a few well-chosen comments in Swahili showed them she was no novice.

The necessary permits and payments were exchanged in the office, and we entered the park and heaved a sigh of relief as the only things that milled around us were animals.

* * *

The annual migration from Serengeti was well under way. Countless thousands of animals had moved from the huge park to the south in Tanzania into this smaller park in Kenya, the two being joined without a boundary fence.

As far as the eye could see there were large open grassland plains with some gently rolling hills, and all the area was scattered with wildebeest interspersed with other antelopes and zebras. Long lines of wildebeest like giant school crocodiles moved in erratic patterns up and down the slopes, noses to tails, blindly following a leader who plainly wasn't going anywhere in particular.

Every now and then a group would take alarm at some imagined threat and explode into a galloping mass of bodies. They flowed like an undulating black sheet over the contours of the slopes until they finally wheeled to a halt, peering with their comically doleful faces to see if there really was any danger.

Our Land Rover likewise wound its way over the hills, passing Keekorok Lodge, one of the two luxurious rest camps of the reserve. It would have been nice to stay there, but we were more likely to be able to poke around if we were living out in the bush.

Eventually we arrived at the official camping area, a cleared oval in long grass near the little river that forms the boundary between Kenya and Tanzania. The site was empty, and knowing from experience which patch would be shaded at the hottest time of day by the only really tall tree, we put up our tent and made camp.

By the time we were organised and had prepared some vegetables for dinner, the sun was getting low and it was time to renew old acquaintances. Leaving a pot of water to keep warm at the edge of the camp fire, we drove to Keekorok Lodge to collect some beer, and then to a camping area reserved for the Wild Horizons Safari Company.

The ranger at the park gate had told Marion that Chegi was now working for Wild Horizons. Chegi was a small, wiry, elderly Kikuyu who had worked for us as cook and general factotum while we'd both been working full time in the field at Masai Mara, and it had been a matter of regret on both sides when we'd had to part. We hadn't had time to let Chegi know we were coming, and we were looking forward to his amazement as we appeared out of the blue.

As we pulled up near the main tent we saw the characteristic silhouette of the small figure with its battered bush hat emerge from one of the tents carrying a bucket.

'Hullo, Chegi,' called Marion. 'Doing a bit of work for once!'

'Ah, was just going to come to camp site to see you,' said Chegi, and went on to empty his bucket in the rubbish pit.

No sign of surprise at all. We looked at each other. The amazement had boomeranged.

'How on earth did you know we were here?' I asked when Chegi returned.

'Ah, Kikuyu know everything, much smarter 'n white

people,' observed Chegi, but I could see he was having trouble suppressing a broad grin. It transpired later that he'd called at the main gate soon after we had, and he'd heard of our arrival from the ranger.

'No customers tonight, Chegi? Didn't they like your cooking?' asked Marion, looking around the otherwise empty camp.

'People not come, only tomorrow,' said Chegi. 'All like my cooking, is better than ever.'

This was unlikely because he'd been unsurpassed as a camp cook even in our day. We accompanied him into the tent, and saw three places already set at the table.

Chegi bustled around for a minute or two, then said:

'Dinner not ready for one hour. I expect you to be late. You always late.'

For the second time I was at a loss for words. I went out to the Land Rover and returned with the beer, and we sat down and exchanged news.

Inevitably the talk turned to the death of Fergus Campbell, for whom Chegi had also worked at one stage.

'Is very bad,' said Chegi. 'Mr Campbell was good man, is very bad.'

'Do you think the Masai did it?' asked Marion.

'Bah!' said Chegi. 'Masai very bad people, but this not right for Masai. But nobody know. Is usually stories in camp because somebody know, but now nobody know.'

Which I thought probably had a message in itself, as Chegi got up to put the finishing touches to the meal.

* * *

We had to spend the night with Chegi because we had no permit to drive in the park after sunset. Next morning, after a nostalgic breakfast of his inimitable camp pancakes, we made our way back to our own campground.

The pot had boiled dry and the fire had gone out, and we noticed the tracks of a large lion that had evidently inspected the camp during the night. It brought back all too clearly my memory of a night a year ago. After too much beer I'd left the tent, and while relieving myself against a nearby bush I'd been enveloped by a roar so powerful that it could be felt as well as heard. I couldn't see the lion, but it must have been less than a hundred metres away; fortunately it must also have been upwind of me. I crept back to the tent as quietly and as fast as I could, and it didn't scent me. After that experience, even back in Britain, I've had a visceral aversion to too much beer at night.

We cleaned up the burnt pan, and had a quick dip in the river which flowed fast enough to be free of bilharzia. Then we thought we'd better get down to some work, so we went to look at the spot where the murder had occurred. Chegi had at least been able to tell us that.

On the way we had a real treat, which reminded us once again of why we were all for the elephants and against the poachers. We rounded a bend in the road, and there was a large group of elephants right in front of us, slowly meandering across the road with a gait that was both lumbering and easy. They browsed occasionally on the way, in no real hurry to go anywhere. Majestic animals, on a scale that no other land animal could match. We stopped the car and watched.

A large male was closest to us, and he looked at us with a certain amount of interest. He towered above us, his head massive, with fine tusks and huge ears. His tiny eyes glistened as he calmly regarded us. Even better, he then flapped his ears out and raised his trunk – a magnificent display by a true giant.

Two in the group were quite young calves. They walked close to their mothers, a mixture of young gangliness and the solemn plod of their elders. From their positions close behind their mothers, they too looked with interest and maybe a little trepidation at us.

When we reached the murder site there was little to see, as I'd expected, but we couldn't think of anywhere else to start. The spot was at the edge of an open area near one of the main rivers of the reserve. As we parked we could hear the barking grunt of hippopotamuses below the bank.

Our permit for fieldwork allowed us to leave our vehicle, so keeping a weather eye towards the source of the grunting we began to wander round. Predictably, we found nothing of significance – indeed nothing at all other than a marker post left by police at what must have been the spot.

After a while Marion called out:

'Nico, where are the large binoculars?'

'Under the front left seat, I think.'

A pause while she peered through them; then:

'What's the name of Pendleton's safari company?'

'I think Ezekiel said it's called Huntsman Safaris now.'

'And what's the emblem that he uses on his vehicles?'

'I don't know – Ezekiel didn't say that.'

'Could it be a black hand clutching a lifted spear?'

'Sounds very likely.'

Marion came round and pointed across the open expanse.

'See over there by the patch of green trees, that must be one of Pendleton's Land Rovers that's stopped, and the driver's been watching us through glasses for ages. He's stopped now that I've been looking at him, but he was definitely watching us.'

'But everybody looks when they see a vehicle that's stopped. It's one of the best ways of finding animals for your party to look at.'

'But not for so long. I've been seeing the sun glinting off his glasses ever since we arrived, and we've been here over ten minutes. It would take him ten seconds to see that we aren't watching animals. Besides, I don't think there are any people in his vehicle.'

'Mm, that is rather odd. Maybe we shouldn't have poked around here quite so obviously. I wonder who the driver is? Why don't we drive down the track past him?'

But as we began to head towards the other Land Rover it moved away rapidly, and we agreed it'd be too pointed to give direct pursuit.

We stopped at a junction, undecided about where to go next, when a Land Cruiser came speeding down a track towards us. It pulled up abruptly when the driver saw who we were. He climbed out, a tall, straight, youngish man in khaki uniform. It was Malcolm Gibson, the park's senior biologist. He'd shown a lot of interest in our projects in the past, and he'd given us a great deal of practical help.

'Hullo,' he called. 'Welcome and all that! I heard you were back.'

The bush telegraph seemed to be in uncomfortably good working order – first Chegi and now Malcolm. Was there anyone who didn't know we were back and poking around? I was glad we'd thought up a plausible reason for having returned. At least I was hoping it would be plausible.

'Hi, Malcolm. How's business?'

'Bit bloody busy at the moment, but not what you'd call useful work. Elephant poachers have been giving us a bad run in the last few months. We're not having much luck catching them or even deterring them, despite having soldiers in to patrol these days.'

'We heard you were having a spot of trouble,' said Marion. I would have kicked her if I'd been near enough – Malcolm might ask us who'd told us that. But he had other things on his mind.

'I'm just going to one now. Did you ever see one when you were here before? If not, why don't you come and have a look!'

Without waiting for a reply he was into his Land Cruiser

and off. It seemed to be at least related to our enquiry, so we swung our vehicle round and followed Malcolm's dust trail up the road.

When we stopped it was in front of a horrible sight: the mountainous grey hulk of a dead elephant slumped on its side, with raw red patches on its head where the tusks had been hacked away. Nearby an African was using a bulldozer to dig a large hole.

Malcolm motioned us towards the carcase. The buzz of flies was audible over the bulldozer, and the smell was potent.

'I have to make notes on the age and sex and condition of all beasts that go this way,' yelled Malcolm over the rumble and roar. 'See if any sort is particularly vulnerable.'

'Do they shoot them?' asked Marion, looking at the injured head.

'No, we might hear that and be after them. Poisoned arrows, usually. Let's see, you can often find the spot...'

He wandered round the carcase peering at the grey skin, then pointed towards a cut in the hide on the rump, which had puffy, septic edges.

'That's it. Once the arrow's gone in it can take up to four days before the elephant's down and unable to move, and the guys track it all that time. When the elephant's incapacitated they hack the tusks straight off. The poor beast isn't dead half the time. It horrifies me every time I see it.'

He dug into the wound with a bush-knife, but found nothing.

'I'm supposed to look for broken-off arrow heads and things as possible evidence, but these lads are too smart. They don't leave a thing.'

'How do they get hold of poison strong enough to knock over an elephant, for heaven's sake?'

Malcolm screwed up his face. 'There are several traditional poisons that the Africans have known for centuries. One's ground-up *Acocanthera*, which is a local shrubby tree from round here. Then there's the *Diamphidia* beetle – they take the guts and the larvae of the beetle and combine them with poisonous tree sap. That combination's highly toxic, but it takes four or five days to fell the elephant. Then there's also the *Strychnos* tree, which grows through a lot of Africa and produces strychnine. No shortage of supplies around here, unfortunately.'

We retreated from the overwhelming sensations of stench and cruelty. Malcolm made another circuit of the body making notes in a small pocket book. As he was finishing the bulldozer drove over towards him, and he gave the driver a wave.

The man moved the machine up to the elephant so that the broad blade was against the back, and then at full throttle began slowly to push the huge lump into the hollow. Finally he drove round the other side and pushed the soil from his excavation back into what remained of the hole. It wasn't a burial to satisfy an undertaker, but the smell abated a little.

'A large old bull again,' said Malcolm as he rejoined us. 'They leave the main herd and they're easier prey for stalking. Not to mention having some of the best tusks.'

'I can only say the very best of luck in catching them or stopping them. I wish there was something we could do to help.'

'Tell people not to buy ivory,' said Malcolm. 'There's no way we – or the elephants – have a chance as long as there's still a market for the stuff.'

He paused, then said: 'Well, I'd better be off to make a report. Why don't you come and have a drink later and tell me what you'll be doing here? I'll probably be in the bar at Keekorok from about five o'clock.'

And again without waiting for a reply he was off.

Marion looked at me, quite fiercely.

'This gives me another damn good reason for wanting to nail Pendleton or whoever it is. I feel quite sickened by the whole business.'

_ 6 _

Later in the day we decided to accept Malcolm's invitation, in case he might have some more information relevant to our mission. We drove to Keekorok, but when we went into the lounge he wasn't there.

However, someone we both recognised as Charles Pendleton was.

After a whispered consultation at the bar we decided it might be worth seeing how a little chat would develop. We took our drinks over to his table.

'Good evening. Mr Pendleton?' I said as politely as I could.

He turned to look at us. He was a tall, solid man, probably overweight but obviously fit. He had large, bronzed hands, but beneath the equal bronze of his complexion there was a slight florid tinge. His most striking feature was a shock of snow-white hair, brushed backwards in waves from his tall forehead, which was reputed to send middle-aged safari females out of their minds. He was likewise reputed to take full advantage of this.

His grey-blue eyes surveyed us.

'Yes.' It was neither friendly nor unfriendly.

'You may not remember us,' I said, and proceeded to explain who we were and what we'd done when we were in Kenya before. I was sure he would know all that perfectly well, but we had to start the conversation somehow.

'Yes,' said Pendleton, without much enthusiasm. 'Think I did come across you once or twice. Remember telling my safaris in those days about the bird nuts they were likely to see around the place. I remember Miss MacTaggart.'

From his tone as he said this last, I thought that he'd probably remembered that the shock of hair hadn't done its trick in her case.

'How's the safari business these days?'

'Not too bad,' said Pendleton noncommittally. 'Money's a bit tight everywhere these days, but there still seem to be enough people to keep a feller in business.'

'Are you still running any of your specialised bird safaris these days?' I tried to make it as nonchalant as I could.

'No,' said Pendleton. 'No, we found there wasn't enough demand to make those pay.' He was looking at us a bit more intently, but perhaps he was only wondering if we wanted to go on one.

'Oh, I heard you did a special one not so long ago for the father of ornithology – Professor Carpenter from the States.'

Comparing notes afterwards, we both said that his eyes narrowed sharply when I said that, and the florid hue became a bit deeper.

'Oh yes, well, that was at Amboseli, but that was just a one-off special. Chap had never been to Africa before and wanted to take some photographs, so he wrote to me from America. Typical scientific blimp. Knew his African birds, though – I was quite surprised.'

'Well, he is supposed to be the best in the world,' said Marion.

'Hm. You'll have to excuse me now. I must be off to check my flock,' said Pendleton. He looked at us with what appeared to be malevolence and left.

'I don't think he wanted to talk about Byron Carpenter,' said Marion, as the large figure receded.

'I don't think he did.'

* * *

We waited a while longer but Malcolm Gibson didn't appear, and eventually we had to get back to the camp before night fell.

While preparing dinner we discussed progress. – or lack of it. Our main achievement to date seemed to have been to have drawn attention to ourselves, including at the site of the murder.

'It isn't as easy as you think,' said Marion. 'In books everybody goes off and makes all sorts of logical investigations, but I'm baffled as to where we should even start with this one.'

'Well, we certainly haven't done much of use yet. But we ought to be able to work *something* out. We're both trained researchers. How about if it was a new research problem we were tackling, and we had to get theories ready for our grant interview?'

Marion glared at me, possibly because her last grant application had been knocked back at the interview stage. However, she was still ahead of me there – my recent applications haven't even been given interviews yet.

'Well, we've got several possibilities as to what happened. Firstly, the murder could have been committed by Charles Pendleton. Secondly, it could have been committed by someone other than Pendleton who works for Huntsman Safaris, thus circumventing the problem of Pendleton's alibi. Or thirdly it could have been committed by someone not in any way connected with Huntsman. Your responses please, Dr Twistleton,' she said with a snaky look at me.

'Well, I guess we have to keep all of these in the back of our minds, but I think I'd dismiss the idea that it was someone not connected in any way with Huntsman. Fergus himself had pointed the finger at Pendleton – Ezekiel just didn't find any of the hard evidence to prove it.'

'Okay, I'll go along with that for the moment. But what about somebody else in Huntsman?'

'We don't know who else is employed by the company – maybe that would be something to find out next. If there was somebody else it would mean that the alibi problem's irrelevant. Pendleton could have organised things by radio or something, without needing to be there in person. However, my reading of Pendleton from my limited acquaintance with him is that he wouldn't trust black Africans with something like that – he'd do it himself to be sure.'

'Mm, that's what Ezekiel said, and I'll go along with that too. D'you remember what Chegi said, that nobody around the camp was talking about the murder? If an African had done it I suspect there'd have been at least a bit of talk around the place.'

'So if Pendleton did do it, what are your views on his alibi, Dr MacTaggart?' Two can play at that game.

'Well, the first possibility is that Pendleton got from Amboseli to the Mara while Carpenter was on his visit, committed the murder and got back. If I remember right it's about three hundred kilometres between the two parks, so the only way he could have done it is by plane. He does have planes, I know, but it would have had to be very tightly organised. Someone would have had to meet him at Mara to take him to where Fergus was, and then get him back to the plane.'

'Yes, and even then it would have taken some hours. Wouldn't Carpenter have noticed that he'd been abandoned for rather a long time?'

'Maybe there was someone else at Amboseli with them? And Pendleton could have come up with some plausible reason – the need to get supplies, or report back to the office or something.'

'Yes, that's something that needs to be checked with Carpenter. I wonder if the FBI knew all of this background when they were questioning him? I bet not.'

'There's one other possibility that we have to consider – that Carpenter is crooked and is in on the whole thing with Pendleton. I know it seems inconceivable, but the old saying is that everyone has their price. Maybe Carpenter even went with Pendleton, or maybe he just knew what was going on and gave the alibi anyway. He could simply have lied about the time that Pendleton left him.'

'So what are you suggesting, that we fly to America and interview Byron Carpenter? Ask him if he's into ivory poaching, and an accessory to murder?'

Marion's lip curled significantly.

'I'm not that stupid. But we just have to bear in mind that the alibi could be flawed. On balance it's very unlikely that Carpenter's part of any poaching ring, but we just have to remember it's a possibility. Maybe he doesn't get paid enough by his university. Maybe he's trying to raise extra funds for his museum, I don't know. Unlikely, yes; impossible, no.'

'So where do we start in all this? Find out who else works for Huntsman and whether they'd be up to killing Fergus?'

'Well, maybe that's a good angle to start on. Someone in the park office should be able to tell us who works for Pendleton and which of them was around when the murder was committed. We'd just have to think up some plausible reason for asking questions like that.'

I broke off as I saw Marion prick up her ears, and then I heard it too. The unmistakable sound of an approaching vehicle engine. And I felt as nervous as she was looking...

* * *

A vehicle coming this late was potentially sinister. Very few vehicles other than official ones had permits to travel after dark, but it would have been most unusual for an administration vehicle to come to the camp site at this hour.

Lights became visible and brighter, and finally swung on to our tent as the vehicle turned into the camping area. We were sitting like rabbits in a spotlight.

'It's probably an assassination squad from Huntsman Safaris,' whispered Marion. 'Watch out for Masai spears!'

'That's not funny. It probably is.'

I was trying to decide whether to suggest we dropped to the ground, when the engine stopped and the lights cut out. The vehicle door opened and a dim figure got out, but the residual dazzle from the headlights made it hard to see detail.

The figure leaned back into the vehicle and began to drag something out. A spear? A shotgun? Worse?

'Sorry to have stood you up earlier,' said Malcolm Gibson.

My adrenalin level began to drop again. I felt a bit silly, though not as silly as I would have if I'd dropped to the ground in front of Malcolm. However, I thought the message about our potential vulnerability was one worth remembering.

'Thought I'd come and make it up to you now,' Malcolm was continuing. 'Louise has taken the kids to Malindi for a week, so I'm temporarily without ties. Don't let me disturb your meal, though,' he added, eyeing off our pots and peelings.

'Not at all,' said Marion. 'Very nice to see you – have some with us?'

'No thanks, I've already eaten in the mess. But perhaps you'll join me in a few of these? I seem to have most of the Mara's dust in my throat as usual.'

He put down the case of beer that he had dragged out of the vehicle, and extracted three bottles.

Marion set the pots on the fire, and we settled down with an open bottle each.

'To tell you the truth it was the bloody poachers that detained me earlier. We had a report of a band seen in the south west corner, but by the time we could get a plane there it was nearly dark. There's a ground party on its way but they won't be able to find much until tomorrow, and if the poachers saw the plane tonight they probably won't be there tomorrow. God, I wish I could make *some* progress against those bastards.'

Marion looked pointedly at me and raised her eyebrows in query. I nodded.

'It's quite a coincidence you should say that, Malcolm,' she said. 'We were just saying the same a few minutes ago. You know we're supposed to be here making a survey of owl populations in the park – well, it was partly an excuse to come and make a few enquiries about Fergus Campbell's death. We found it hard to accept the official version of that.'

Malcolm looked at us with unusually wide eyes. 'Well, you devious pair! And I thought it was our beautiful birds that had brought you back. But I'd have to say that you're not the only ones who don't believe the bullshit in the papers about Fergus's death. Do you have any idea what the real story might be, though?'

Marion explained in some detail what Ezekiel had told us. It was something of a risk, but I think both of us would have vouched for Malcolm any time.

Malcolm listened without a word. When Marion had finished he took out a pipe, and still in silence he packed it and lit it. Finally he spoke.

'What you've suggested would certainly fit in with our knowledge. The poachers seem to be getting good information on where the elephants are, and who would know that better than a safari leader driving round all day looking for animals?'

'Can't you find out incriminating evidence from the poachers? Or haven't you ever caught any?'

'Oh yes, we've had a few, but the operation is always much too carefully organised. The poachers themselves are Somalis from the far north. They're met by an African contact outside the park who passes them information and tells them where to return with the ivory, again outside the park. They have no idea who the man is, and the rendezvous differs on each occasion. They put the ivory in a truck with covered number plates, and the man pays them off in cash. End of contact. We tried to set up a trap once with some poachers that we'd caught, but they almost certainly took us to the wrong rendezvous.'

'But how could the information be passed quickly

enough through all these channels? Elephants do move around.'

'Well, Pendleton has two or three powerful radios. He could call up a contact outside the park very quickly and pass a coded reference. We sometimes pick up weird radio messages that make no sense at all, of a strength suggesting a local transmitter. And the contact only has to point the Somalis in the vague direction – they're ace trackers, those guys, and they soon pick up the trail.'

'What happens to the ivory after that?'

'That's a good question, and I wish we knew the answer. The ultimate destination could be one of several areas. A lot of ivory goes to the Far East, to be carved and sold in places like Hong Kong, Japan and mainland China, and a surprising lot still goes to Europe. Especially France, which isn't as fussy as some countries about checking the documentation of origin. It's also possible that some goes to South Africa, for reshipment from there to Botswana. Ivory is still sold in South Africa but under heavy restrictions, whereas in Botswana any amount can be sold legally. We've been putting pressure on the Botswana government to stop this, but there are a lot of powerful white trading voices in the country and we've had no effect so far. And Botswana needs the income from the rich visitors who come in via South Africa.'

'Couldn't you intercept the ivory while it's still in Kenya?'

Malcolm snorted even more loudly than before.

'Don't think we haven't tried! A huge amount of effort's

gone into trying to do just that, but we still haven't any idea of how and where they're moving it around the country. We've kept a very sharp watch at ports like Mombasa, we've had snap raids on trucks going down to the coast, we've tried all sorts of things, and we've never picked up a damn thing. It's not as though tusks are the sort of things you can hide, either. A good one can weigh up to fifty kilos and be a couple of metres long, not to mention being curved which makes it even harder to pack away. It's possible of course that they're being taken over the border into Tanzania and down to Dar-es-Salaam, but the Tanzanian authorities have been keeping their eyes pretty wide open, and they haven't found anything either. Whoever's doing it has got a very professional operation going, but then of course there's a lot of money at stake.'

'How much is the ivory actually worth?'

'Well, at the moment I think they can get around thirty-five pounds sterling a kilo if they sell it to the right dealer. Which means that a single good elephant could be worth a couple of thousand pounds to them. They could never make that sort of income any other way – no wonder the poor beasts don't stand a chance. That's why I said to you earlier that as long as ivory can be sold anywhere legally and without limit we'll never stop the poaching.'

'The British papers are saying that some African countries are arguing for legal but controlled ivory harvesting and selling, to give local villagers an income and also an incentive to keep elephant numbers going. Couldn't that work?'

'I suppose in theory it could, though when it's been tried by villagers who are also crop farmers, the elephants have trampled all the crops and the farmers are worse off. But you said one key phrase – "legal and controlled". There's just too much corruption and too many people wanting to make huge fortunes and damn the consequences. The movement of ivory's already controlled at the moment, but you get situations like Burundi which over the last ten years has exported three hundred tonnes of ivory with appropriate certificates, and yet its total elephant population last year was one animal – and that's if the animal hadn't wandered back over the border into the Congo. The ivory would have mostly been poached in the Congo, and maybe in other nearby countries, and Burundi has provided corrupt cer-tification. The latest estimate that I heard was that about fifty per cent of the ivory trade is correctly certified and the remaining fifty per cent's poached.'

'Is it mostly old, lone males that are being killed?' asked Marion. 'I guess that wouldn't have too much impact on herds as a whole, would it?'

'Yes and no. Yes, if they're truly old and lone bulls there's not so much effect, but some of them are in fact the active and dominant males of a herd, so once they've been killed they're not there to mate with the females. Recent surveys are showing a marked decline in male numbers, and that's got to be having an effect. And no, it's not only males that are taken. Some females have pretty reasonable tusks, and some poachers are not fussy. And taking out mothers has a major impact. If a calf loses its mother when it's two years old or less it'll always die. If it's between two and five years it's only got a thirty per cent chance of making it, and even at six to ten years old it's only about a fifty per cent chance. That's why I have to collect all that data on the carcases – to try to get a better handle on what's happening to the elephants as a whole.

'I can't remember all the stats that I've read, but I can give you a couple that horrified me. Here in Kenya there were estimated to be 130,000 elephants in 1973, and only around 40,000 last year. And the overall African elephant population's gone from 1.3 million to 625,000 in the last ten years. Halved in a decade – you just can't keep a rate of decline like that going.'

'It's all deeply depressing,' said Marion, 'But coming back to Fergus's death for a moment, we just told you Pendleton claimed to be at Amboseli at the time with Professor Carpenter, but is there anyone else employed by Huntsman Safaris who might have killed Fergus? That way there's no problem with the alibi.'

'He doesn't have any European staff working for him, and most of his Africans are fairly menial and wouldn't be able to stage a carefully planned murder. However, he does have one more senior staff person. I don't really know him, but his name's Peter Motokwe and he's supposed to be quite smart. Probably pretty ruthless as well. He'd certainly be a contender if he was around in Mara at the time.'

'Okay, now for the practicalities of Pendleton doing

it himself. You know he has a plane. Would it have been feasible for him to have left Carpenter long enough to fly it here and back to do the deed? What about refuelling, and do the parks keep records of flights in and out of them?'

Malcolm thought for a moment.

'With the plane he's got he could easily do the return trip without refuelling. He has an arrangement to draw fuel from park supplies when he needs it, but even if you checked and found that he'd used a lot around that period you could never prove anything. He often takes members of his tours up for game spotting – he'd just say he'd used it for that.'

'What about flight records?'

'Well, Pendleton's supposed to keep his own, of course, but they could easily be fudged. The parks keep a log of flights that are notified by air traffic control from Nairobi or wherever, but with regular old hands like Pendleton there's no recording of joyrides once he's arrived. And of course there are no radars to check planes flying in and out. So the answer's yes, it would have been quite possible for him to have done it. He would have run a risk of the plane being seen if he landed on the official Mara strip, but there are a number of other places where an experienced pilot who knew the ground could land without much chance of anyone seeing him. It's not allowed, of course, but he could always say it was an emergency landing. He'd be stranded without transport, though – he'd have to have arranged for someone to meet him. I'd say the whole thing would be possible, but the organisation would have had to have been very tight and Professor Carpenter would surely have noticed if he'd been left for quite a few hours?'

'Well, we don't know how closely the FBI questioned him on points like that – they wouldn't have had the background you've just outlined to us, so it may not have occurred to them to look for a matter of lost hours. It might be worth following up, but then again Professor Carpenter probably wouldn't remember in sufficient detail at this stage.'

'It could just be worth checking the records at Amboseli, though,' said Malcolm. 'You might get a lucky break. As it happens I'm flying down there tomorrow – why don't you come along and we'll see if we can discover anything?'

Oh no. Not a flight in a small plane…

_7_

There was a striking sunrise next morning, as a bright pink glow spread behind jumbled clouds scudding across the sky. We were up in good time to see it because Malcolm was leaving early for Amboseli, but I wasn't in any mood to appreciate it. I tried to persuade Marion to abstain from breakfast given the blustery conditions, but that advice was not at all well received. Marion never had any problem.

We drove to the airstrip and found Malcolm already in the plane checking his instruments. I squeezed into the rear seat in the hope that I would see less there. Marion climbed into the front beside Malcolm.

As the plane warmed up Malcolm turned to us and yelled: 'I want to have a look at any herds of elephant we see along the way. If you spot any give me a shout and I'll go down for a closer look!'

It was getting worse by the minute...

I'd brought an empty plastic bag with me and I put it very accessibly in front of me. I braced myself as the plane took off, weathered the sudden changes of angle, and then found I was actually enjoying the ride as we cruised over the rolling hills speckled with animals. It just showed that having no breakfast was solving the problem.

Until the first elephants came into view, that is. Malcolm pointed to our right and suddenly, before I'd even focused on the herd, the plane fell sideways, its stall warning bleeping insistently, and my stomach was left somewhere in the sky.

We levelled out not very far above the elephants, but I'd already lost all interest in game. I gripped the wall handle, gritted my teeth, and tried to pretend it was a roller coaster. Then I remembered that roller coasters made me sick as well, so I grabbed the plastic bag and was.

We circled the herd a couple of times and then returned to our cruising altitude, where I slowly began to feel human again. Briefly.... Marion had spotted some more elephants. No sooner had she tapped Malcolm on the arm than we were into another sickening plunge – a death dive if I was lucky.

I began to wish the poachers had eradicated all elephants from Africa and we wouldn't have to go through all of this. Maybe Marion would also be struck blind and wouldn't see any more elephants; maybe I could sue the plane's manufacturers for assault.... Stupidly I opened my eyes at one point, and found we'd flipped through ninety degrees and I was looking through the side window directly at the ground. I closed them again with a prayer for quick salvation.

Salvation came, but it took a while. Eventually, with a series of bumps we taxied to a halt at Amboseli. I staggered out of the plane, and wondered why the ground was moving up and down. I looked at Marion to see how she had fared. She was saying to Malcolm: 'That was marvellous – I haven't enjoyed myself so much for ages! Oh, Nico, you do look white – you should have had some breakfast after all.'

It simply wasn't fair.

* * *

At the administration offices I had to sit down with some strong black coffee, so Marion and Malcolm left me and went to conduct Malcolm's business. They were also going to try and take a not too obvious look at the logs of aeroplane movements.

They rejoined me in the bar just before lunch. I tried to sound enthusiastic about life and asked:

'Anything exciting?'

'Well, it's there,' said Marion. 'An entry on the correct day for Pendleton's plane arriving from Nairobi. The only thing even faintly out of the ordinary is that it says 'plane delayed' in the remarks column.'

'Which happens fairly often,' said Malcolm. 'There were quite a few others like it in the book. Lots of people flying in this country can't or don't stick to schedules. Professor Carpenter's plane could have been late in from America or wherever if he was being met directly. Or Pendleton could have been waiting for stores or something. I'm often awry on my schedules.'

'So we're back where we started.' I was rapidly losing enthusiasm for life, the investigation, everything.

'Not quite,' replied Malcolm. 'It's extra confirmation that his plane was here at the correct time. In the subsequent entries there's no record of it going off on any trips, until the last day when it's recorded as leaving for Nairobi again.'

'End of record – all clean and above board,' added Marion. 'His alibi's better than when we started. Though as Malcolm said yesterday it wouldn't have been impossible for him to sneak a trip away without the flight being recorded. I wonder if Professor Carpenter *would* remember if he was ever left alone during the safari? I wish we could somehow meet...'

Marion's voice had tailed off, and she was looking at a third person who was standing near us and listening – an African, who must have edged along the bar towards us. As soon as he realised he had been noticed he quickly walked out.

'Who the hell was that?' I asked.

'I have a horrible feeling that I know,' said Malcolm. He called to the barman. 'Maxwell, who was that near us at the bar just then?'

'Oh, him Peter Motokwe,' replied the barman. 'He work for Huntsman Safaris.'

We looked at each other.

'Shit,' said Marion.

There wasn't much we could do about it except be more careful in future, but it put rather a dampener on the conversation. Malcolm finished his drink and went off to attend to more business, while Marion and I drifted off to look for some lunch. I could only face a bit of fruit, but Marion as usual ate enough sandwiches for both of us.

* * *

Afterwards we wandered around the rest camp area, having no vehicle to go anywhere else, when to our great delight we ran into an old friend. Jerry Szymanowski is one of the resident biologists of Amboseli. Originally an American, he now considers himself an East African, and anyone who knows him couldn't imagine him living anywhere but in an African game park.

He hasn't been known to visit a city for years, having the necessities of life sent to him from Nairobi, but despite this he's remarkably knowledgeable on world affairs. He also has one of Kenya's better private libraries in his camp bungalow. Although most of his work is on mammals, he's also a bird fanatic and shared many exciting and uncomfortable hours in the bush with us in the past.

'Waal, how about that!' exclaimed Jerry. He didn't sound like an East African yet. 'I heard you were around.'

Not another one. Was there anyone in Kenya who didn't know we were here?

'I guess you came out specially from England to see the Madagascar squacco?'

'Why, has one turned up again?' asked Marion.

The Madagascar Squacco Heron is a rare bird in East Africa, but we'd once before seen one in Amboseli where these birds are occasional visitors.

'Yeah, there was a report of one this morning in the Loginya Swamps. I was just goin' out for a look. Hitch a ride!'

We looked at each other.

'I suppose we'd better see when Malcolm's likely to be leaving,' I said reluctantly, and went back into the main office.

It turned out that Malcolm wasn't likely to be finished before dark, so we all piled into the front of Jerry's Land Cruiser and set off. There was about as much dust inside the vehicle as on the surrounding roads, but that too was like old times. The taste of African dust is an essential part of any ornithological expedition.

We arrived at the swamps and parked at a vantage point overlooking the spot where the squacco had been seen, but there was no immediate sign of it. We had a nice view of two saddlebill storks, tall, angular and handsome, stepping slowly through the vegetation looking for food, and also of the rare long-toed lapwing, a plover with big feet so that it can run over floating mats of vegetation like a lily-trotter. But no Madagascar squacco.

We gradually became restless as biting insects from the swamp began to invade the Land Cruiser.

'Did Byron Carpenter manage to see a Madagascar squacco while he was here?' Marion asked Jerry.

'No idea. I never saw a whisker of him in all the time he was here,' replied Jerry. He sounded rather put out.

'What?' exclaimed Nicholas. 'Didn't Pendleton bring him over to see you?'

'Nope. I was dyin' to see him and chat about birds – he was my professor back in the States, you know. But not a one of us even saw his shadow.' The memory clearly rankled.

'How extraordinary,' said Marion. 'What on earth was Pendleton up to?'

'Well, he hates my guts and me his. But you'd still have thought he'd have brought him over for a chat with all of us. He could have earned his money for even less effort then. I'll bet he stung old Byron for a good few bucks.'

'Most peculiar...' Marion was still frowning.

'By the way, do you know one of Pendleton's men called Peter Motokwe?' I asked.

'Yeah. Another one where the gut instinct ain't good. Wouldn't trust him in a fit of Sundays.' Jerry hadn't lost his talent for bizarre phrases.

He paused.

'He's a lot smarter than most of the Africans round here, by the way. He's not a local. I think I heard he comes from Botswana originally but he spent a while working in South Africa, as a powder-monkey in a gold mine on the Rand. He speaks Setswana, English, Afrikaans and Swahili that I know of – probably a few others as well. He's even got his pilot's licence since he's been working for Huntsman. They reckon he does a lot of wheeling and dealing over tourist souvenirs round here, but nothing illegal's ever been pinned on him. But I sure got a strong feeling about him.'

At that moment the conversation was interrupted by the arrival of a squacco heron, but after careful inspection through binoculars we decided it was an ordinary squacco not the Madagascar one. By then the biting insects were attacking in droves, so we called it a day and drove back to the camp.

* * *

By the time Malcolm had finished his work it was too dark to fly back to Masai Mara. We fetched the sleeping bags we'd thrown into the plane as a precaution, and went to find an empty hut in the rest camp.

We flew back early the next morning, and I was much relieved that Malcolm was in a hurry and didn't want to check elephants or any other animals. Or have breakfast....

Back at our own camp we'd just climbed out of our Land Rover when Marion called out:

'Nico, come and have a look at this!'

I went over, and she pointed to a stretch of tyre mark in the dirt that led into unmarked dust.

'Someone's been here and tried to obliterate their tracks, but they missed that little bit.'

We moved carefully towards our tent, peering at the ground. There were no tracks anywhere, not even our own from the day before.

Inside the tent nothing seemed to have changed, though in what was rather a jumble it was hard to be sure.

'I think someone's been poking around to see what we're up to,' said Marion.

'Could have been raiders looking for something to pinch. They're always coming over from Tanzania, and we're right on the border.'

'Don't be stupid, Nico – there'd be nothing left here if it was bandits. All this stuff is saleable, the tent included. They wouldn't bother to hide their tracks, either. I think someone's getting interested in what we might be doing here.'

It was a rather uncomfortable thought. We were used to the intrigues and back-stabbings of Faculty Board meetings, but this was moving into a very different league.

_ 8 _

Negative thoughts were also passing through Charles Pendleton's mind. He lay back on a cane reclining lounge in his large tent, his legs stretched out and his hand conveniently near a tumbler, an ice bucket and bottle of scotch on a side table. He sipped at the whisky, and he thought.

It was maddening really, because it had all been going so well. There'd been that policeman, true, but he'd been disposed of in a neat way, and there was no risk of that being pinned on anyone. Not even a Masai, unfortunately. But now there are these two snooping biologists. Somehow – God knows how – they seem to be guessing altogether too much about what's gone on. They will have to go.

He considered the options for a while. He probably shouldn't risk a disposal like the previous one – circumstances were not likely to be as suitable again, and there were two instead of one this time, which would make it harder. It would be pushing his luck to try that again, but there must be something. There must be some way...

An idea came to him with the third glass of whisky. He

would provide a little diversion. It would keep them out of the way for a reasonable time, and with luck it might deter them altogether. And if they accepted the bait they would incriminate themselves beyond doubt. Then if they returned he'd have no hesitation in arranging appropriate treatment.

He drained the glass and walked over to his desk. The smile on his face was not nice.

_ 9 _

The day seemed long and hot. It was all the more irritating because without having said it I think we both felt we were now wasting our time at Masai Mara.

We drove around rather aimlessly, looking at birds here and there, but without any real purpose it soon became boring. We opted out earlier than usual, and withdrew to the bar of Keekorok Lodge. At least it was cooler there, but there still didn't seem to be much to talk about.

Marion was roused from her state of torpor when an African walked slowly past our table. He wasn't looking at us, but she stared at him, then whispered to me:

'Isn't that Motokwe or whoever?'

I looked over at the man and nodded.

We began to watch him as surreptitiously as we could. I'm sure we weren't so naïve as to think he'd suddenly reveal evidence that he or his employer had murdered Fergus Campbell, but there wasn't much else to do anyway.

Peter Motokwe was carrying a loose wallet stuffed with papers, which he placed on the bar while he ordered a couple of bottles of beer. As he felt in his shirt pocket for money his elbow caught the wallet and knocked it to the floor. Papers spread and began to flutter in the breeze. Motokwe swore and stamped his foot on some to catch them, then bent down and moved to retrieve them from the various corners to which they were drifting. This done he gave money to the barman with a surly comment, picked up the beer bottles and strode out.

Marion looked at me.

'He's missed one of his papers, you know. It's caught between the bar stool and the counter. I'd love to know what's on it...'

She went to the bar to order another beer, dropped her change as she picked it up, and collected both paper and change as she fumbled on the floor.

She returned to our table, cautiously opened the folded paper and read it. Her eyes widened, and she passed it to me without comment.

It was a pink duplicate or triplicate counterfoil. There was no billhead, but in rough carbon copy typing it read:

Delivery to: Ebony and Ivory, 209 Kilindini Road
                 Mombasa
Qty: 60 kg

The docket bore a serial number 0931, and printed across the bottom of the form it said 'Terms Cash 14 days'.

Neither of us said anything for some moments; then Marion spoke.

'I can't see what else this could be except a shipment of poached ivory to an outlet of Pendleton's in Mombasa. It's probably one of those shops that sells carved souvenirs to tourists.'

'Yes, the name's probably a hangover from when you could sell ivory legally in Kenya, whenever that was.'

'They might well still sell it under the counter if they were sure the customer wasn't the police.'

'So how about we go down to Mombasa and check it out? We *might* even be able to pick up an incriminating purchase.'

'Not to mention a good curry or two...'

It really took no persuasion at all, and we left the bar with distinctly lighter steps.

* * *

Peter Motokwe returned to the bar a little later to buy some more beer. He noted that the paper had gone, and he left the bar in a much better humour on that occasion.

_ 10 _

It was a long and not very exciting drive next day from
Masai Mara to Mombasa. We went through Nairobi and
Voi, and interminable dry farming country in which farmers
seemed to be doing little more than scratching a living. If
that. There was also the worry that the Marstons' old Land
Rover wasn't really up to such a long trip any more. It had
certainly developed extra rattles by way of protest. The sight
of Mombasa came as quite a relief, even if the all-encom-
passing humid heat didn't.

We checked in at a small hotel that we'd stayed at on
previous visits. It hadn't changed at all, which was unfortunate given that it had needed major renovation even then.
However, it was a cheap and convenient base.

'Hurry up and get showered,' said Marion. 'I'm dying to
see if Suleiman's still doing his goat curry.'

Marion thought of food a lot of the time.

As we went out it seemed a good idea to drive past
Ebony and Ivory while it was closed, to have a preliminary
look at it without our curiosity being too conspicuous.

Number 209 was at the sleazier end of Kilindini Road, near the docks. However, when we got there it certainly wasn't shut, and it wasn't a tourist souvenir shop either. It was a doorway with a flashing red and blue neon sign over it reading:

Ebony and Ivory
Live Entertainment

The doorway was very much open. Music could be heard coming from it, and the lights inside were only partially obscured by a black woman lounging against the door frame smoking. Every now and then she shifted her position, which produced interesting ripples in the short and tight dress she was wearing.

Marion and I looked at each other.

'Curry?' said Marion.

We drove on.

We veered right at the end of Kilindini Road, past the large godowns of the port, past the oil terminal, and right again into Jomo Kenyatta Avenue which took us back to the town. At least Suleiman's was the same as it always had been. So was Marion's goat curry, and the Chicken Vindaloo which I couldn't resist any time I saw it on a menu.

With a certain amount of choking induced by chilli, we discussed the Ebony and Ivory.

'D'you think we've been had?' asked Marion.

'I was just wondering that. Not necessarily. It was our

assumption that it would be a tourist shop. I can't see why a seedy nightclub shouldn't also sell illegal ivory, in fact it might be quite an appropriate sort of place.'

Marion sniffed, or perhaps it was just the chilli again. 'It looked seedy all right, but I'm not so sure about the ivory.'

'Well, there's one way to find out...'

Marion stared at me – the sort of stare that meant trouble. 'You're not proposing to *go* there, are you?'

'I'm not, but I'm suggesting we are. There should be safety in numbers in a place like that.'

'It'll be disgusting. I wouldn't be seen dead in a place like that. You just want to go and look at naked females.'

'I'm doing it for Fergus – we both are, if you remember.' I assured myself that any naked females would be purely incidental.

'They wouldn't let women in, would they?'

'There are plenty in there already by the look of the place.'

'Christ, Nico! You know what I mean.'

'Well, I don't see why not. You might be some loose woman I've picked up and we're going off for a good time before whatever... Hell, I don't know. I've never been in a place like that before. All I know is that I'd be prepared to go in with you, but I'm damn sure I'm not going in alone.'

Marion glared at me even harder before conceding.

'I suppose we'll have to give it a go. We can only get thrown out. I hope.'

After the curry we drove back down Kilindini Road,

parked at a discreet distance from the Ebony and Ivory, and approached the door. A different black woman stood there, if anything more tightly and scantily clad than the earlier one.

Marion pushed me to the front.

'Halloooo, big boy,' said the woman, in a rich, deep voice. She held out her hand as though to shake mine, but at the last moment dropped it and grabbed me in the crotch. 'Ha! Ha, ha, ha! Yo' wan' come in wid yo' lady frien'?' She sounded like a bad American movie.

'Yeah, we thought we'd come and see the show,' I said, trying to sound like a man of the world. Unsuccessfully.

The woman cast a not very flattering glance at Marion. I didn't dare look at Marion's return expression. The woman should have already turned to stone or ice by now.

'You go pay de man.'

We went over to the solid – and fully dressed – black man that she'd indicated, and negotiated an entrance fee. It was a lot more than I'd expected, and undoubtedly more than any of the entertainment would be worth.

Inside was the typical night club of a B movie: cheap tables and chairs scattered round a dimly lit floor, smoke and general stuffiness and a smell of alcohol, relatively unclothed waitresses and an almost entirely male clientele. Many already well lubricated by the sound of their voices.

A few musicians sat at the edge of a more brightly lit stage at the back, and a man at a microphone in the front was announcing that Bella Donna would be singin' fo' de guys, and maybe if everyone was lucky, doin' a little dancin'.

A roll of drums preceded the entry of Bella, wearing high heels, a G-string and a feather boa. A few artful twists of the boa made it clear she was not wearing anything else. She sang a slow number while she undulated suggestively around the stage, teetering several times at the front edge as though to fall into the laps of some delighted men at a front table. She appeared to be having trouble keeping her bosom confined in the boa. She had a lithe if ample body, and a fine voice that might have been good enough to give her a career as a blues singer. A rather sad waste.

As we were being served with drinks the tempo suddenly hotted up. Bella flung away the boa and began a tap dance which caused the whole of her body to shake, her breasts moving like two large blancmanges. The whistling almost drowned out the music.

The music stopped, and Bella announced: 'Ah'm tired now. Ah think ah'll go an' lie down on mah bed….'

It wasn't clear whether that was an invitation or not. A couple of people left the room, but possibly to wee or go home or something.

The band played nondescript music for a few more minutes, and then the man was back at the microphone.

'Guys, this is the moment you've all bin waitin' for! Let me introduce to you – Amazing Grace!'

It took me only microseconds to work out in what way Grace was Amazing, as she sashayed across the stage. Water melons didn't come into it – she was quite grotesquely bosomed. She came forward and tilted herself towards the various tables – she was probably trying to bow, but at the same time trying not to overbalance, gravity being what it is.

'There's some good-lookin' guys in here tonight – and ah'm thirrrsty...'

The compere appeared with a long glass like a yard of ale, but filled with water. Drinking this required Grace to arch back to an amazing extent, presenting further insights to students of her anatomy. In the course of the drink much of the water trickled down her neck and over her body, giving it a superb dark brown sheen. Then she yelled at the audience:

'Any you guys thirsty? Yo' like to drink at de fountain?'

There was an immediate eruption of hands from one table. They obviously knew what to expect.

'Hey, you! Big boy...' Grace pointed at one from the table, and he came a little unsteadily on to the stage. The compere brought out a jug of water which Grace rested on one shoulder.

'Down, big boy!' She pointed at the floor in front of her, and the man went down on his knees facing her. She adjusted her position slightly, then tilted the jug so that the water ran down the front of her shoulder, down her right breast, and trickled off the nipple as a thin fountain. The man, already goggling at the sight with an inane grin, began to slurp the water. Grace kept moving slightly so that the man had to come closer to catch the liquid, and finally his mouth came into contact with the nipple.

'*Naughty* boy!' yelled Grace, swung her breast to one side, then brought it sharply back so that it smacked the man on the right side of the face. At which he overbalanced, to roars from his friends, and Grace tipped the rest of the jug over him.

'God Almighty,' said Marion. 'Is this what men find exciting?'

'Not me,' I said, lying through my teeth. 'Perhaps we'd better make some enquiries about ivory before we get too far embroiled.'

I waved a hostess over.

'I wondered if it might be possible to buy some ivory here?'

The waitress gave me a rather surprised look. She glanced at Marion.

'Yeah, but is only Sarah on today fo' de ivory. Is plenty of ebony yo' can choose from. But what yo' want a girl fo'?'

She looked at Marion again.

I was going to pay for this when Marion got me outside again.

'No, I didn't mean that,' I said, feeling myself getting pinker by the minute. I was wishing Marion had vetoed my stupid idea more firmly. 'I heard that it might be possible to buy some carved ivory souvenirs here?'

'Don' know 'bout dat, sir. I ask de boss.'

She went to a dinner-jacketed white man who was sitting at the back of the room surveying the general proceedings. He got up and came over to our table. The jacket that had looked smart at a distance was shabby and fading.

'Mercy tells me you have some trouble...?'

'No trouble, no. I'd heard that it might be possible to buy some ivory souvenirs here, and I might be interested.'

'*Really?*' said the man. 'Who told you that?'

I should have been readier for the question. 'I heard from someone in the hotel. We were talking about souvenirs and this man said he'd heard you had some ivory.' It sounded lame even to me.

'And which hotel would that have been?' The man was looking at us with a curious expression.

I thought a little faster this time. 'Well, the hotel doesn't matter because he was only a casual visitor there, but it was the Regent actually.'

I wasn't having anyone following us to the actual hotel where we were staying.

'I see,' said the manager, and his tone suggested he saw a lot more than I'd been telling him. 'I'm sorry to say we don't sell any of that type of souvenir here at all. But anyway you must know that the sale of ivory is not allowed in Kenya – it's completely illegal. We are an entirely legitimate house of entertainment.'

'I'm sorry. The man must have heard about the Ivory in your name and jumped to the wrong conclusion, I guess.'

'Ah yes,' said the manager, as though such a thought would never have occurred to him. 'That must be it. I'm so sorry we can't help you.' With another sideways look at us, he went back to his table.

We finished our drinks soon after. I won't bother repeating what Marion said when we got outside. I'm still trying to blot it out of my mind.

* * *

After they had gone, the manager got up again and went to the phone in his office. He dialled a Nairobi number, and when it answered he said:

'There were two people here tonight asking about ivory. They matched the description I was given. They're staying at the Regent Hotel.' And he hung up.

However, the discreet surveillance later at the Regent Hotel was unable to find the same couple. Nicholas and Marion won that one at least.

_ 11 _

It hadn't been a good start to the new, scientifically based investigation.

I'd made a fool of myself the previous night. I was also uneasy about the manager's odd reactions to my questions. It was almost as though he'd been playing with me.

Marion was convinced we'd been set up by Peter Motokwe. I was trying to keep an open mind, but I had to admit that a set-up seemed plausible. Either way there was no point in staying longer in Mombasa, but there didn't seem much point in returning to Masai Mara either so we drove back to the Marstons.

* * *

Late that evening the children were in bed, and we sat with Monika and Peter on the verandah of the house. We told them about our abortive attempts to play detective. I was still in disgrace after Ebony and Ivory, so Marion took the running.

'As I see it there are two things left that could still provide useful information. One would be for us to chat to Professor Carpenter. We might just see significance in something that the FBI would miss because they didn't have the local background. And on the off-chance that he is crooked himself, we might just notice if he gave anything away. But short of flying ourselves over to America I can't see how we could do that. The other would be to poke around in Pendleton's own tent at the Huntsman camp. There might be *something* that would provide a clue, but I can't for the life of me see how we could gain legitimate access to do that.'

I said: 'I know one way. If you're female and willing it's very easy to get in there. I've done my bit in the night club – it's your turn, Marion.' In for a penny, in for a pound.

If looks could have killed I'd have been hyena meat. 'You don't seriously expect me to waggle my eyelashes and hips at that creep, do you? Apart from questions of my taste in men – which is rapidly going off you, by the way – I've refused Pendleton twice in the past. Now that he knows we're interested in Fergus Campbell, don't you think he's going to be just a teensy bit suspicious?'

Marion had an answer for everything.

There was silence for a moment, then Monika said thoughtfully: 'I wonder if Sophia is in need of a holiday...?'

She turned to Marion. 'Sophia is white and used to be a part-time prostitute in Nairobi. I knew her well when I was doing social work. She's respectable and more or less retired these days, though I believe she's still ready to oblige old friends. She's a mature but attractive woman, and looks just about the sort who would go on a safari and fall for a great white hunter. I don't think she's so well off these days, but if you were prepared to pay for her to go on one of Mr Pendleton's safaris I'm sure she'd be able to see plenty of the inside of his tent. She'd probably enjoy the holiday.'

We discussed the idea for a bit. I was worried it might do more harm than good, like my own attempts, but the others were more enthusiastic. We agreed that Monika could at least arrange for us to meet Sophia so we could judge the prospects.

Meeting her entailed another wild ride through the hills down to Nairobi, and another coffee at the Thorn Tree. But when we finally met her, any remaining reservations disappeared.

I wondered afterwards what sort of person I'd been expecting. Certainly someone more vulgar than the good-looking and cheerful woman of middle age who confronted us. A slight tendency to make ribald comments, perhaps, but more importantly she seemed a person with presence of mind who would be as likely as any to carry out the mission successfully. If there was anything to be discovered, that was.

We'd agreed beforehand just to tell her that Pendleton was suspected of illegal ivory trading, and to look out for any signs that he was in contact with dealers and such like. She readily agreed to the idea.

She gave me a broad grin. 'I haven't had a good holiday

in ages, dear. It'll do me the world of good.'

I gave her enough cash to book a week's safari plus some spending money. Her eyes twinkled as she took it.

'Reminds me of the old days, taking this off you, though I *never* charged that much...!'

I could sense Marion coming to the boil again....

Sophia went off to the safari office to make her reservation, and rang us later to report that she'd been able to get a place on the following week's safari.

There was nothing to do then but to wait.

_ 12 _

SOPHIA

You never know what life's going to bring you. One minute I'm retired from what I like to think of as the hospitality industry, and suddenly I'm in demand again. And all expenses paid – that makes a nice change.

It's funny – in all the time I've been in Africa, I've never been on a safari. Never really been interested – lots of antelopes all looking the same. But now that it's happening I'm actually interested to see what it's like.

I got my ticket from a little office in Nairobi. I had visions of me sitting up through the roof of a Land Rover, surveying the lions and cheetahs in best Hollywood style, but it turns out that it's a small bus, a bit like the ones that run around Nairobi. Never mind – the Hollywood producers don't seem to be here at the moment either.

Our bus isn't the fastest transport on the road. It's overtaking the Masai herders, but only just. However, that gives me a chance to look at the other passengers and judge my chances of getting into bed with the tour leader. Who we haven't seen yet, by the way – he must be somewhere in Masai Mara.

I'm one of fourteen on the tour. Three couples – shouldn't be any problem there, though you never know. Three guys by themselves, which leaves four women besides me who appear to be unattached. Three of them don't look like much opposition if I play my cards right – the last one we'll just have to see. Maybe one of the single guys will step in anyway.

* * *

It actually wasn't too bad a drive after all. The antelopes weren't all the same, and we saw two cheetahs standing on a hillock and posing in their beautiful fur coats. When you saw them you'd wonder why any human would take animal fur like that and wear it – there's just no comparison.

The camp doesn't look too bad. I've got my own small tent with a camp bed, and plenty of warm blankets. There's a tent for meals, and the cooking smells drifting over the camp-site are quite appetising.

Even more appetising is Mr Pendleton, the tour leader, who we've now met. A big man with a quiet sense of power about him. He stands straight and moves well, though he's probably a bit overweight now. Also a bit too ruddy in the face – probably drinks a bit. But his crowning glory's his mane of white hair, swept up and back with a beautiful wave in it. He probably thinks a bit too much of himself. That's fine – that should play into my hands.

* * *

One day touring round the game park – it wasn't too bad, but I'm not here to look at animals. I did like the elephants, though – they were even bigger and mightier than I'd expected, but they could still move with surprising grace.

Last night I chatted a bit to Charlie as I like to think of him, though he seems to prefer being called Charles. At least it's not Mr Pendleton. He was telling us of some of his unusual encounters with big game in the park, which gave me a chance to look adoringly at him. I don't think I overdid it, and he was looking at me quite speculatively by the end of the evening. Tonight might be the first move.

* * *

My main opposition, Chloe, has also been making eyes at Charlie, but I think my eyes might be winning. I put on a figure-hugging blouse this morning, and there's more of me to hug than Chloe has.

At the end of the afternoon, as people were dispersing back to their tents, Charlie came up to me and murmured: 'I'm sorry that we haven't the staff to run a bar and offer more than the glass of wine that you have with dinner. Would you be interested to drop in to my tent after dinner and share a glass of something a bit stronger?'

Would I indeed! After dinner I wandered over as casually as I could manage, and put my head into his tent. He was *sitting reading through some papers, but he waved me in to a seat next to him. Something stronger turned out to be a rather nice whisky, and we chatted about this and that while I cast some casual glances around the tent and its layout.*

It was a large tent, well set up and furnished. We were in a sitting area with two comfortable arm chairs, a small lounge and a coffee table. Back and to one side was an office desk, a chair and a filing cabinet. Various papers were strewn on the desk and skewered by a spike on top of the desk. In the other back area of the tent was a partition, which presumably screened his sleeping area.

I was always discreet with my clients, so I will simply say that the evening developed very well, and I believe an equally good time was had by both. I was very late back to my tent, seen by nobody I hope.

* * *

On the next evening Charlie missed dinner as he had to go to the park offices for some business. I contemplated trying to sneak into his tent to look at his papers as Monika and her friends had asked me to do, but the door flap was securely tied up and the African assistant was keeping too much of an eye on the camp site in his master's absence. However, on the following evening I was invited into Charlie's tent again after dinner.

We weren't long into the first whisky, when there was a

commotion outside the door flap and the African assistant called out: 'Baas, there's a problem with Mr Lawson – he says he's sick.'

Charlie didn't look too pleased. 'Wait here a moment, would you? I can't believe this is anything much – he seemed perfectly well at dinner.'

He got up and left the tent. This was my opportunity, and I quickly got up and went over to the desk. I couldn't rummage too much or he'd see that somebody'd been into the papers, and none of them was exposed enough to show anything useful. However, I had a quick look at the items on the spike. Two of them were possibly of interest, and I memorised them as much as I could. I didn't have any paper with me, but I could write them down when I got back to my tent.

It was unfortunate that I was still standing near the desk when Charlie suddenly came back into the tent. His eyes narrowed considerably when he saw me there.

'Was there something you wanted?' he asked, much less friendly than before.

I couldn't think of any good excuse, so I came up with a feeble one. 'I was getting stiff sitting down, and I wasn't sure how long you'd be.' At least he hadn't seen me too close to the desk.

'Hm, well, we might just finish our drinks, and then I have some work I have to do for tomorrow.'

So I was dismissed. The next evening I noticed that he invited Chloe for a drink after dinner, and I think she got back to her tent pretty late as well. I think I was right out of favour then. I just hoped that the names that I picked up might be what Monika's friends wanted.

_ 13 _

The days began to drag as we waited for Sophia, but then we had our first stroke of luck.

Peter Marston was sitting on the verandah sipping beer and opening his day's mail from the research station when he called out:

'Did you say the American who came out on Pendleton's trip was called Byron Carpenter?'

'Yes, why?' replied Marion.

Peter handed her a notice from the Biological Society of Southern Africa, which gave members who'd enrolled for the Annual General Meeting a program for the sessions.

'I'd forgotten all about this,' said Peter. 'I'm a member of the society, and Monika and I put our names down ages ago to attend. It's coming up in four weeks' time, but it's in Johannesburg and I won't be able to go. Our Director's going to be away and I'll have to run the station while he's gone. The interesting thing is the name of the guest speaker at the Scientific Session – it wasn't known when they sent out the preliminary notice.'

I looked over Marion's shoulder and read that the guest speaker would be Professor Byron J. Carpenter, Curator of the Beaglehole Museum of Ornithology, who would address the meeting on: 'Parallel Evolution among the Bird Faunas of Different Continents'.

'I've already paid for both of us, and I haven't done anything about cancelling it because I'd forgotten all about it,' continued Peter. 'Would the two of you like to go in our places? It's supposed to be for members and spouses only, but Dirk Pienaar who's organising it is a friend of mine, and if I give you a note for him saying I've sent you as last-minute substitutes he'll be only too pleased not to have to alter his hotel arrangements.'

Marion gave me a very intent look. No was not likely to be an option.

'We should certainly go if we can afford it,' she said. 'It's the perfect opportunity to ask Carpenter about his visit to Amboseli, and at least we'll feel we're *doing* something again!'

Marion was not one for kicking her heels.

'We could check out air fares in Nairobi tomorrow. There might be some cheap flights or something.'

'I don't think you'll find much between here and South Africa,' said Peter. 'You'll be lucky to get a direct flight at all. I believe Lufthansa or Swissair does one, but you'll probably have to go via Malawi or Zimbabwe. Kenya doesn't exactly encourage people to go and visit the Boers.'

'Well, we can only go and see. I suppose we'll need visas

for South Africa. Do they have an Embassy in Nairobi – I guess not?'

'You must be joking. No, their business is handled by the British High Commission if I remember right. You'd better ask there.'

'While we're down there we'll also be close to Botswana,' said Marion. 'That's where Malcolm told us that ivory's still traded legally in large quantities. It might be worth poking round there a bit too. Unless Nico feels he's done enough hunting for ivory souvenirs?' she added nastily.

I didn't dignify that with a response.

Next day we went into Nairobi to check out prospects. With British passports we didn't need visas for Botswana, and the South African visas would take until the day Sophia returned from her safari. We booked flights to Johannesburg for two days after that.

* * *

The further wait was frustrating, but we got hold of various travel books and brochures and spent time poring over those. After that we felt we were experts on southern African roads, travel and general geography – which was to come in quite handy later on.

The day finally came when Sophia was due to return from the safari. We had arranged to meet her in Nairobi the next day to find out if our investment in her trip had paid off.

Over the inevitable coffee at the Thorn Tree she told us she'd managed to gain access to Pendleton's tent on two evenings.

'I got to see quite a bit of it, all in all,' she said. 'It's very big, with a sitting area in one part and then a large bed section half screened off. On one side of the sitting area is a sideboard full of booze, and at the back there's a desk. I was never in a safe enough situation to be able to try the drawers or anything, but there was a spike of receipts standing on the desk. The top one was from...' – she consulted a slip of paper in her handbag – 'Botswana Trophy Services, PO Box 83, Lobatse.

'All it said on it was 253 kg. No price or description or anything. The ones underneath I couldn't see, except that one was stuck on crooked and was half exposed. It said Swaziland Import-Export Co., and there was a place name that started off S-I-T-E, but I don't think that was the full name.

'And that was all I could find out, I'm afraid. Charlie-boy didn't believe in leaving people alone in his tent, especially not the opposite sex. He only went out for a few minutes when one of the other tour people was reported as being sick, and unfortunately he came back while I was still standing near the desk. I wasn't in an incriminating position, but he went quite cool on me after that.

'It was a good holiday, though...' She looked dreamy for a moment. 'If you ever want me to do any more of that sort of checking I'll be more than happy!'

So Lobatse was added to our Botswana itinerary. We looked at our road map of South Africa, which included Swaziland adjacent to the Transvaal, and guessed that the place name of the Swaziland Import-Export Co. was probably Siteki in the east of the country. That too might repay a visit in due course.

_ 14 _

Two days later we were actually on our way.

As the plane began to descend towards Jan Smuts Airport in Johannesburg, I have to admit that I felt a tightening of the stomach muscles at what South Africa would actually be like. Marion and I had always liked black Africa and black Africans, despite some frustrations, so we tended to regard South Africa and apartheid like the Pope probably regards the Antichrist. I'd never conceived of circumstances in which I might remotely want to visit the country, and yet here I was descending into its very heart.

I peered across Marion's front at the view through the cabin window, but all I could see was a grey-brown haze. As buildings became discernible through the haze it was rather like coming down to an industrial English town – rows of suburban houses, cooling towers of power stations, spreads of factories. Only the parched brown or burnt black earth showed it wasn't Europe, though it didn't look much like Africa either.

We disembarked, passed through an impersonally

efficient passport control and a thorough Customs check, and made our way into the main arrival hall. I looked around, and found that whatever I'd been expecting it wasn't this.

I'd thought there might have been a majority of rugged white South Africans going aggressively about their business, with a few menial black Africans hovering around the edges. After all, it was supposed to be a white country.

What I saw was a few rugged whites, but they weren't doing anything very aggressive. After that it was almost as diverse as Heathrow. There were a few very un-rugged blazers and cravats, more British than the British. There was a group of beautifully manicured young men who seemed to be very close friends. There were what looked like European migrants; there were orthodox Jews with yarmulkes on their heads, and even a rabbi.

A group of Indian men were lined up facing a wall. It looked at first like a security check, but when they all knelt on the floor it was evident that they'd been lining up to face Mecca. There were women in saris, a few Chinese, and there were black Africans – hundreds of them. One or two were well-dressed men with briefcases and umbrellas, who scurried across the floor. Some others had menial jobs, but there was no sense of cringing around the edges – they were as much a part of the overall throng as any. More so, in fact, because of their colourful variety. Some were singing, some were shouting, one was engaged in banter with a white supervisor. Men wore their sloppy uniforms with defiant panache, and the variety of outrageous headgear that went with them was certainly not provided by officialdom.

African women also wandered to and fro, blankets wrapped around their waists, sometimes enfolding an infant, and with parcels on their colourfully turbaned heads. It wasn't entirely Africa as I knew it, but it certainly wasn't Europe. Above all, it was vibrant.

Our priorities now were to cash some travellers' cheques and hire a car. The first was quickly done, but the second entailed a half hour wait while a car was brought from the firm's city office, the airport supply having run out. I bought a copy of the Rand Daily Mail and sat down, while Marion went to see if any of the airport shops sold her brand of face-powder.

I read the front-page story about disruption caused by the latest strikes in Britain. Was there a hint of malicious glee in the tone of the article? And another on how in Australia the Queensland government still had legislation restricting movement of aborigines outside their reserves within the state. There was no editorial comment about this, but perhaps it was not by chance that the column imme-diately beside it carried a report of a speech by Australia's representative at the United Nations, denouncing apartheid and the South African government's plans for independent black homelands.

Then I turned to page three, and began to read an account of the inquest on Ezekiel Mphephu. Ezekiel had fallen from the fifth floor of John Vorster Square, the South African

Police headquarters in Johannesburg, while being questioned about alleged membership of the African National Congress. A police witness gave evidence that Mphephu had suddenly leapt from his chair and rushed towards the window that was half open for ventilation, its bars temporarily removed for repairs. He had tried to escape along a ledge, but had fallen.

Counsel for Mphephu's family had produced a witness who testified that while sweeping the courtyard within the station he had seen Mphephu hanging screaming from the window, held by ropes around his ankles. He was there for some minutes before his captors pulled him in again. Counsel for the police dismissed as unreliable such evidence from a man who had recently been sacked from his job at the station.

A police surgeon testified that Mphephu had died of injuries consistent with falling on to a hard surface from a considerable height. A pathologist who had conducted an independent autopsy for the family noted that Mphephu had burn marks on his genitals, and additional lacerations that were not accounted for by a fall. In particular there were lacerated rings around the ankles consistent with prolonged pressure from stout ropes.

The police surgeon, recalled, gave his opinion that these marks were caused when Mphephu scrambled over the window sill. A verdict of suicide was returned. The newspaper noted that this was the thirty-fifth death in police custody in the previous twelve months.

I remembered now why I'd never wanted to come to South Africa, and I felt sick. Sick at the transparency of what had obviously happened, sick at the fact that justice was not remotely done, sick that in a few minutes I could already have begun to feel this country might not be as bad as it was made out to be. Even sick that the Africans should be going around so cheerfully when this sort of thing was occurring. I wondered why they didn't try to do something about it, until I realised that Ezekiel Mphephu probably had been doing just that. At least the country had a free press still able to report that sort of thing, but how much better to be a free country in which it didn't happen in the first place.

Marion returned having failed to find any face-powder, and we went back to the Avis desk to see if our car had arrived. It had, and we signed the necessary papers and paid the deposit.

'David will take you to your car,' said the elegant young lady, in her clipped voice. It came out more like 'Dyvid wull tike yuh to yuh caw'. A young African in a red overall ushered us towards the door and out into the car park, where he unlocked a Mazda hatchback and showed us the controls. He spoke entirely to me, with a deferential politeness that wasn't quite matched by his eyes which suggested that while he was playing by the rules he didn't necessarily accept them. He kept calling me 'Baas'. I wanted to shake him and say 'Stop calling me that – I'm not your boss!'. Except that in the circumstances I was.

David lifted our cases into the luggage compartment.

'Can we give you a lift anywhere?' I was determined to stick to my own principles of equality.

David looked slightly hesitant. 'You going to city, baas?' he asked tentatively.

'Er, I don't actually know which way we're going. We want to go to Lobatse in Botswana.'

David's eyes lit up. 'Ah, Botswana is very good place. I come from Botswana. Yes, you take me into city and I show you the road for Botswana!'

This proved a good move, because David was able to navigate us out of the airport's maze of weaving under-passes and overpasses, and advise on lane-switching on the motorway to Johannesburg to avoid mistakes at the inter-changes. As we sped along, the city skyline came into view – tall, modern office buildings much like any other large city, but with a distinctive frame of flat-topped 'mountains' of spoil from the gold mines that came right up to the city's edge. To the right we could see a tall telecommunications tower, and then a ridge of natural rock that – at 6000 feet, I read later – must have been the crest of the Witwatersrand, the reef that gives the whole area its name.

The motorway ended at somewhere called Bedfordview, and the road narrowed a little as we passed the Eastgate shopping centre, then drove among older suburban houses like those I'd seen from the plane. Then into the city proper, where we were particularly glad of David's guidance. All the trucks seemed to be driven by Africans, with the same verve and intermittent lunacy that was characteristic of independent African countries.

David pulled us in at a point on the south edge of the central city area, where a ramp led up to an overhead motorway.

'You go up there and follow M2 West and then Krugersdorp. Then you go through Koster and Swartruggens and Zeerust and then you get to Botswana.' He grinned at us. 'Dankie, m'baas. I hope you enjoy your journey!'

How funny. The passport and customs officers who belonged here hadn't wished us a good stay, yet this man who is a half-stranger here does so. Maybe the atmosphere of this country is a distillation of an endless array of paradoxes.

_ 15 _

We set off along the motorway, which soon terminated and left us driving through a sprawl of dormitory areas of Johannesburg. According to our map Soweto lay only just to the south of us, but curiously few signs pointed towards it and we could see nothing of it from the road. Maybe officialdom didn't want to admit that it existed.

We meandered on through intermittently hilly country, dull brown dormant pastures interspersed with equally dull fields of dead mealies. At intervals the dead grass had been burnt off the fields, leaving only boulders and termite mounds standing in blackened landscapes of lunar barrenness.

The towns, uninteresting as they were, came as positive relief. Small and old, they were like stone replicas of Wild West towns, each with its slightly colonnaded main street of a few shops, a bank, an insurance office, a church and several pubs, and a couple of dusty side streets running off. It was a bit like passing through a railway station in a train; you had hardly registered that it was there than you were back in the countryside again.

Eventually we arrived at Zeerust. Seeing from the hours listed on the back of our road map that we wouldn't reach the Botswana frontier before the border gates closed, we decided to spend the night in Zeerust.

We drove several times up and down the main street, which was a little grander than those of the towns we'd passed through earlier. We soon realised that the only decision to be made was which of the four old hotels would be the least uncomfortable for the night.

It probably made little difference. The one we picked had a dark, musty room with an old brass bed, the sagging mattress of which offered a night of unavoidable together-ness beneath its torn and rust-spotted mosquito net.

The room had a small washbasin with a cold tap in one corner. We went to use the shower in the bathroom down the corridor and found the water cold. When we mentioned this at the desk the woman said: 'Ag, the boy hasn't stoked up the fire yet. I'll get him to do it just now.'

Later we heard the sound of shovelling. Looking out into the hotel yard from our bedroom window we saw the 'boy', a grizzled black man at least 75 years of age. He made up for his evening tardiness by starting the morning shovelling at 4 a.m.

The sulphurous smoke that drifted into our room drove us early to the lounge, where a rather unenthusiastic waiter brought us drinks. He delivered the change to me on his tray, having pointedly pulled his tip out of the pile of coins as a precaution against my possible ungenerosity.

Later we were summoned to the dining room by a prolonged outbreak of fevered African drumming. This turned out to be the elderly furnace boy again, and the drumming must have been the high point of his evening.

The meal consisted, amazingly, of six separate small courses followed by coffee. A red-jacketed waiter wearing white gloves served them, bringing the Afrikaans version of the menu to us between each course. The menu anyway seemed a formality, because it was table d'hôte so he brought the next course in sequence whatever our response was. He appeared not to understand any English, but he tried very hard. It was probably his first job since he came in from the kraal, and he couldn't have been at it for more than a day or two.

He brought one soup plate at a time to our table, walking very slowly and placing it carefully on the table before removing his gloved thumb from the soup. The soup stain was later joined by white sauce, gravy and custard as other courses appeared, and was only saved from being joined by coffee because that was self-service in the lounge.

Marion looked at me towards the end. 'I really don't know whether to laugh or cry,' she said. 'He means well, and he's trying *so* hard. I guess it's a clash of cultures. He's expected to be a British footman from the turn of the century.'

The one thing you could say for the hotel was that it was cheap, but next morning after a four-course breakfast we weren't sorry to be packing up and moving on.

I carried our cases down the back stairs into the yard,

trying not to be seen by the furnace boy in case he should turn out also to be the porter. Marion walked down the main street in a further attempt to get some face-powder. She came back to report she'd managed to get something vaguely acceptable, from stock that she felt the chemist must have bought up in case Queen Victoria ever visited the town. Which unfortunately she hadn't.

* * *

And so we were off again. It should have been another fifty kilometres to the border, but after scarcely more than twenty we were surprised to find ourselves passing of signs warning of an approaching frontier. On enquiry at the brand new South African border post we discovered we were about to enter one of the many fragments of the independent black homeland of Bophutatswana. We filled in our long bilingual exit forms and handed them in, then drove a short way down the road to an identical border post building where we filled in trilingual Bophutatswanan entry forms of similar length, indeed of remarkably similar layout and printing. One might almost have wondered about collusion between these two separate countries...

We had our passports stamped by the Taolo ya Dipase-poroto, then continued for twenty minutes down a dusty gravel road, dodging chickens, goats, African children, men on bicycles, and women carrying loads of firewood on their heads, until we came to another border post, clearly the old

South African one. Once again there were trilingual exit forms to be filled in at length, and passports to be stamped. Then, having contributed so handsomely to the Records Department of the Republic of Bophutatswana during our twenty-minute visit to the country, we drove a little further to a sign welcoming us to Botswana.

Our sighs of relief were a little muted as we were presented in the border post with bilingual entry forms.

'Bloody hell,' said Marion. 'We should get the Nobel Prize for Literature for this.'

But at least we were in Botswana, and as we quickly discovered, almost in Lobatse too. We seemed scarcely to have left the border post than the town was spreading out before us, a group of dusty buildings nestling in a dry and dusty valley. We crossed the railway line, then turned right into the main street and cruised along looking for any sign of Botswana Trophy Services. We found nothing, and the Botswana Telephone Directory at the Post Office merely gave 'Lobatse' as the firm's address, so we called at the Police Station.

The station officer gave us a rather odd look, and told us it was about fifteen kilometres out along the Ghanzi road. We headed off that way through sparse, thorny vegetation, our progress quite slow because the road was very sandy. We were also travelling in counter-flow to an enormous herd of cattle being driven down the road, and they were spread all over it. They must have been coming from something marked on the map as the Ghanzi Farms, and were no doubt destined for an abattoir in Lobatse.

Ragged Tswana herdsmen, with thick woolly caps and heavy woollen jackets, plodded barefoot in the dust alongside a mongrel assortment of lean and bony cattle, wild horns pointing in all directions. The men had small bags slung on leather straps, and carried long wooden poles. When not prodding the cattle the men held the poles across their shoulders and hooked their arms around them. The long column of animals was raising a small dust storm, and we almost missed the sign directing us down a side turning to Botswana Trophy Services.

The premises of the company were most unprepossessing, a collection of tin-roofed sheds with open, slatted sides. I could see why the policeman had been surprised at our enquiry – it was clearly not a place that expected tourists. Still, now we were here we might as well try to make something out of it.

We went up to a small hut that looked like an office built on to one end of a shed, but it was empty. At that moment a tall, muscular black man wearing only shorts came out of a shed pushing a dripping wheelbarrow full of wet animal hides that wobbled like jellies. Marion asked him where the manager was and he nodded at the second shed.

The rank and pungent smell of tanning, already strong outside, was much worse inside. The shed was festooned with hanging skins of all sorts, some wet, some dry, some clean, some dirty. Against the wall stood slabs of stiff elephant hide, like rows of wooden boards. Two Africans were stirring vats of murky liquid, and a figure near them looked on closer inspection as though he might have been a white man.

He came over to us and motioned us back outside the door.

'Ja?' Not friendly. He was a large man, muscled beneath some flab, wearing only a very dirty singlet and stained shorts. His body too was covered in smears that did not bear too much examination. His bare feet were large and horny.

'We were interested to know if you had any ivory for sale,' said Nicholas.

'Who told you to come here?' asked the man in a rather belligerent tone.

'Nobody really,' said Marion quickly. She was probably trying to stop me doing another Mombasa act. 'We came across your name in the telephone directory while we were in Lobatse, so we thought we'd call in on the off-chance. But I can see you only deal in skins here.'

'Ag, ja,' said the man, seeming to ease off slightly on the hostility. 'You'll have to go to our retail place which is up at Maun. We don't sell anything down here because visitors don't come this way much. They're all going to the swamps. This place started as a plant to process skins from safaris hunting in the Kalahari, and it's just convenient to keep it going for that sort of operation. No, I'm afraid you'll have to go to the showroom at Maun. There's nothing at Lobatse at all.'

I'd been looking at the road map. 'I see we can get to

Maun if we go on up this road through Ghanzi and Lake Ngami.'

The man gave us and our car a withering look.

'Not in that tin can, you can't!' he said scornfully. 'You need high clearance and four-wheel drive, and even then you usually get stuck. It's through the Kalahari sand. You'll have to go back to Lobatse and through Francistown.'

Without another word he turned away and left us.

'Friendly type,' said Marion, as we climbed into the car. 'And I used to think Pendleton was churlish!'

_ 16 _

There was nothing for it but to go to Maun. The trip took us the best part of the next two days, driving through uninteresting dry scrub and past little settlements beside railway halts. They had musical names like Mosomane, Mmamabula and Moreomabele, which belied their sad dustiness. Only Francistown possessed a little style.

From there our road went north-west across salt pans in very arid country, but as we crossed the northern edge of the huge Makgadikgadi Pans we stopped to wonder at the sight. Dry, rough brown land gave way to a narrow strip of dried grass, then a band of encrusted salt, and then a huge expanse of water that seemed almost like looking out to sea. On it and in it were great flocks of flamingos and pelicans, which made up for all the dry brown land before it.

Maun also made up for a lot: a pleasant, rambling town of sandy streets, built mainly of circular African huts with thatched roofs, standing in neat groups surrounded by stockades. Woven mats and vividly coloured washing hung around them, and plump African women plodded between them carrying cooking pots and buckets, conversing volubly and scolding their children. Tall shade trees offered relief to the landscape and the inhabitants.

We found accommodation at the safari camp just north of the town. The streams and rivers running out of the Okavango Delta made the countryside greener and more wooded than the rest that we had driven through. It was a peaceful oasis, and as we discovered towards dusk a beautiful one, with a vivid orange sunset reflected over a wide expanse of water, completely still in the calm of the evening.

The centre of Maun, as far as there was one, was marked by scattered government offices, a police station, post office and school, and a garage, bottle store and hotel.

Interspersed with these older buildings were some uglier and intrusive new ones, housing sellers of souvenirs to the many visitors who come to see the Okavango Swamps. From their size this was evidently big business, and among them was a building the size of a small warehouse labelled Botswana Trophy Services.

This branch did at least expect visitors, and a tour bus parked outside suggested that it had some. However, when we entered the reception area it was deserted. Its only feature was a static and very uninspiring display of goods. At one end was a pile of assorted hides and some mounted animal heads, and for the rest glass cases showed leather goods like handbags, wallets, purses and key-tags, some roughly carved wooden shields and spears and masks, and a miscellany of carvings and jewellery made from verdite, tiger's eye, malachite and ivory. Each item was ticketed with a code number, and a price expressed in Botswanan pulas, South African rands, pounds sterling and US dollars.

I peered at the display, trying to get inspired. 'It's no wonder there's nobody in here. This is the most boring and uninviting display I've ever seen. Nobody'd be tempted to buy anything from this.'

'It certainly doesn't look like a thriving way of disposing of lots of ivory,' said Marion.

But as she spoke, a door in one corner marked 'Private' opened to disgorge what was evidently the tour party. They came out chattering with great animation, holding order forms which they marked with the code numbers shown in the display cases. They handed these in at a window marked 'Reception', which had opened up as they trooped out.

Money was handed over in exchange for vouchers, and they lined up at a second window marked 'Delivery', where in five minutes or so the various items they were purchasing were inspected, wrapped and labelled and handed over.

Then they all left, the windows closed down, and we were left standing in silence once more, amid the dusty museum display.

'Let's go and have a drink,' said Marion. 'It might give us a bit of inspiration.'

We went back to the safari camp, and sat on the patio outside the bar overlooking the river, sipping refreshingly cold beer while the occasional dugout canoe paddled or poled its way past.

'It looks as though the interesting bits of Botswana Trophy Services are all at the back,' said Marion.

'Which you have to be on a tour to get into, as far as I can see.'

'Perhaps we could think up some reason. Why don't we say we're thinking of organising safaris up here and we'd like to check on facilities that are available to them? That would give us a good excuse to look everywhere and ask plenty of questions.'

'Mm, that's not a bad idea. Let's go back after lunch and give it a try.'

On our return we rang a bell beside the 'Reception' window, which was opened in a moment by an African girl. We explained our story and she offered to fetch the manager, who appeared shortly after through the 'Private' door. He was a short, rather weedy man, somewhere in his thirties, who couldn't have been born far from the sound of Bow bells. I instinctively disliked his manner, which was half obsequious and half challenging.

'The girl tells me you're thinkin' of runnin' safaris up 'ere?'

He was rubbing his hands, apparently unconsciously.

'Yes, we're investigating the possibility and we wondered what sort of facilities were available to be included in an itinerary. For most people the chance to buy good souvenirs is as important as any part of the trip. Must impress the folks back home, eh!' I thought I might as well bung it on – he looked the sort.

He was. 'Ah, well, you've come to the right place for that, because we certainly understand what people like. We've got a very good operation goin' 'ere. You probably noticed 'ow well it went this mornin' – I believe you were standin' out 'ere when the Afrofari party came through.'

It was a statement, not a question. Keen eyes, watch your step with him, I thought.

'Yes, it was very impressive, actually. You must have been showing them your range of goods in the back, because they all seemed to know what they wanted when they came out.'

'Yer, well, it's good salesmanship, innit? It gets their interest up seein' all the stuff bein' made, and they like to go back and say they actually watched the native craftsman doin' it. It takes about 'alf an hour to go round, so they've got plenty of time to think about it. Tell you what, I'll take you round and show you the set-up, and then I'll let you know our terms at the end.'

Terms, I thought?

The 'Private' door led down a short passage between two rooms marked 'Office' and 'Store', and out into an open area which was the main part of the warehouse. This was like a giant and very active craft studio. Several benches were occupied by African women marking and cutting leather, and further on their pieces were being sewn into bags, wallets and other items by more women, at machines or stitching by hand. Yet others were labelling the finished products with the name of the skin that had been used, and stacking them on to a trolley.

In another section men at benches were working on lengths of wood. They had an assortment of hand-tools, and also some neat electric equipment for cutting and turning the wood.

'We usually make sure the men are doin' some of the 'and-carvin' while the parties are goin' round,' said the manager. 'It sounds better than machine tools for tellin' the folks back 'ome.'

Then they came to the bench where a solitary African was carving ivory, which proved to be the most fascinating of all the operations quite apart from our interest in the subject. He too had smaller versions of the cutting and turning equipment, but the unexpected object was a small dentist's drill with a wide array of drill bits, and he was using this most skilfully for carving designs into the shaped piece of ivory.

'It's too 'ard to do any other way,' said the manager. 'I mean, you can do it by 'and, of course, but we'd be sellin' about one piece a year an' it would cost a small fortune. It's expensive enough as it is.'

'Where do you get all the ivory from?' I asked it as casually as I could.

'It's all local,' said the manager sharply. 'All our stuff's local. There's still unlimited 'untin' in Botswana outside the National Park areas.'

Marion had been lagging all the way, probably because she couldn't stand the manager. I knew her views on sleazes. She had particularly stayed behind to watch the ivory carver, no doubt fascinated at the delicacy of his work. I wouldn't have minded watching him for longer, but the manager dragged me on to the verdite and malachite carving and the jewellery setting. She rejoined us just as the manager was outlining his terms to me.

'Now, we're offerin' the stuff at the prices you saw outside which are quite competitive with anybody else in this area, and we're throwin' in the tour round 'ere as well. So it's a good deal for them, and for you too because each time you bring a party 'ere you and the little lady can buy anythin' you like from our stock at fifty per cent discount. As much as you like – no limit. Now that's quite an offer, innit?'

'Yes, I'll say,' I said. 'You must have a good mark-up to be able to offer that.'

The manager gave me a dirty look and sniffed.

'Yer, well, let's say we can manage,' he said.

I had obviously breached commercial etiquette by mentioning such a thing.

'Now, that's not all,' continued the manager, brightening to his sales pitch again. 'If you bring a party that spends more than six 'undred pounds or eleven 'undred rand between them on one visit there'll be a nice little present in it for the lady wife. Could even be one o' those bits of ivory you was admirin' so much, darlin'' he said, leering at Marion. I was surprised that she didn't disembowel him, or worse.

Jesus, I thought – there really must be some money in this game. But before either of us could respond to this magnanimous offer we were distracted by a most unfortunate happening. A side door into the shed opened and an African walked in. He glanced at our little group, then stopped dead in his tracks and stared at us with a frown growing on his face. Finally he went into the office, gesturing urgently at the manager to join him as he did.

Through the office window we could see the manager and the African in heated conversation, in the course of which the pair stared out of the window at us several times. I couldn't think why the man's face should ring a bell, but Marion unfortunately did.

'Christ,' she whispered. 'I've just realised who that is! It's Peter Motokwe, the one who works for Huntsman Safaris and was listening in to our conversation in Amboseli that day. What the hell would he be doing in Botswana?'

'Well, he comes from Botswana,' I replied, trying to keep my voice down. 'Jerry told us that. But I can't believe it's just an unlucky coincidence that's brought him in here. He must be involved in all this somehow. But it's certainly dropped us in it. I can imagine word for word what he's saying to the manager in there. Do you think we should do a quick bunk?'

'Certainly not,' said Marion. 'We've done nothing wrong. They can't prove that we aren't planning to bring safaris here. In fact their response might be a measure of their guilty conscience. Leave it to me.'

A moment later the manager returned, and he was clearly angry.

'I believe you've been 'avin' me on. You're not safari

operators but scientists or somethin". He made scientists sound like criminal frauds. 'Perhaps you'd like to explain.'

He was glaring at us and I noticed he was standing firmly between us and the door.

I was desperately trying to think of something to say, when Marion stepped in with what I like to call her puffer-fish display. She drew herself up to her full five foot two, which manages to look like six foot when she's fully aroused and angry, and she addressed the manager in her haughtiest Edinburgh Scottish.

'I'm not exactly clear what being scientists has to do with it. We are indeed, but I was not aware that that prevents us from running safaris. In fact as biologists I should think we'll be able to do it rather well. My father is just retiring as an Under Secretary in the Foreign Office, and he wants to maintain his interest in Africa. He is thinking of investing his capital in a safari company, with us doing the running of it. As you're doubtless aware it's a profitable business, and we'll make a lot more money at it than in science.'

I must remember to congratulate Dr MacTaggart on his promotion next time we're in Scotland. He had recently retired from his medical practice in Inverness, and was probably at this moment fly-fishing on his favourite river. But he would definitely forgive his daughter for this misappropriation of his name. He shared most of her genes.

The manager was effectively wrong-footed. He now knew very well that we were scientists who'd been snooping in Kenya after ivory poachers, and he didn't for a moment believe we had any intention of running safaris. He probably also knew that most of his ivory was not Botswanan and a lot of it was Kenyan, but he couldn't question us further without implicitly admitting such things.

'Ah, well, that's all right then, innit?' he said rather lamely. 'Well, I'll be lettin' you on your way, then, but don't forget our terms if you ever bring any safaris up this way.' Slight venom in the last bit, and unnecessary emphasis on the word *if*.

'We shall consider your offer in relation to those of other operators in the district,' said Marion, with acid sweetness. 'Come, Nicholas!'

We departed with as much dignity as we could muster, pointedly not looking in the office window at Peter Motokwe.

* * *

As we got into the car I said: 'Phew, you got us out of that nicely. Next time I see your father I'll congratulate him on the way he's bred his daughter, as well as on his new appointment.'

'You don't know the half of it, laddie,' replied Marion. She was having trouble getting out of the Edinburgh mode. 'Get going and I'll tell you more.'

As we drove down the road she said:

'You know when I stayed back to watch the African carving ivory. Well, I asked him if he ever carved whole tusks, thinking of those ones you see in oriental airport shops and so on. He said no, he only ever got pieces of tusk to do, and he pulled out a wooden box from beside his workbench to show me. It contained sections of tusk about a foot long, each individually wrapped in polythene bags.'

'That's rather odd. Why would it be done like that?'

'Well, I had an idea when he pulled out one of the pieces in its bag. As he undid the bag several green coffee beans rolled out on to the bench. I stared at them and asked how on earth they got there, and he laughed and said 'Oh, they're always there. I collect them for a while and then I sell them.''

'Go on,' I said. I was still trying to make sense of the puzzle.

'The wooden box was the sort like a tea chest that coffee beans are shipped in. It had had a name and address on the side painted over, and SIECO stencilled on top. Any guesses about that?'

I thought for a moment. 'The 'S' might just stand for Swaziland?'

She nodded.

'And the 'IECO' for Import Export Company?'

'Uh-huh.'

'Hm, sounds plausible. But where does that get us?'

'As far as I know Swaziland doesn't produce any coffee, but Kenya does. We know that the authorities in Kenya have never managed to intercept poached ivory in transit, but they've probably been looking for awkward packages containing entire tusks. What if the tusks were cut into sections, wrapped and placed inside shipments of coffee beans being exported from the country?'

'But that would rather ruin the tusks, wouldn't it?'

'Why? They're going to be cut anyway. You saw the sort of things being produced. They're quite small, most of them. Very few tusks'd ever be carved whole. They could cut the sections a lot smaller than they do without it mattering.'

'True. But there's another thing. Ivory's a lot heavier than coffee beans for its volume. Wouldn't port authorities become suspicious about shipments where the cases weighed much more than normal?'

'Mm, hadn't thought of that.'

She pondered for a minute or two, then said:

'Well, it depends how much care they put into it. We've got the impression it's a well-run operation. They could be sending out quite a few cases, each with only a few sections of tusk in so that the weight's not increased hugely, and if they're really smart they could counterbalance the tusk weight with a few other plastic bags containing polystyrene beads or something equally light. In fact they wouldn't want too much of anything other than coffee in each box, so that if Customs men open it all they see is beans.'

'I guess it would be possible. But coffee's expensive stuff to use just as packing like that. They'd waste an awful lot.'

'Who said anything about wasting it? You take out the ivory and pack it all into one or two boxes, top up the coffee in the others, and re-export the coffee elsewhere. After all, it's called an import-export company – what better?'

'Well, there's an equal possibility that the ivory's legally obtained, and someone's just using old coffee boxes to ship it without cleaning them out properly. But it does seem a bit odd, I grant you. Could it be a good enough reason to visit Swaziland and see the sights of Siteki?'

'You betcha,' said Marion. 'I think we've done Botswana for the moment. I'd rather put a bit of distance between ourselves and Peter Motokwe or we might get done as well.'

Back at the safari park we looked at maps to work out the best way to get from Botswana to Swaziland. It seemed to be through Potgietersrus and Middelburg in the central Transvaal. The map didn't show any more homeland borders to be crossed, but then it hadn't shown Bophutatswana on the way to Botswana either.

Marion was peering more closely at the map.

'If we go this way,' she said, pointing out a fairly large diversion, 'we could visit Jan.'

'Jan?'

'You remember Jan du Toit. I've told you about him before. He went out with my sister Moira for a while when he was at Aberdeen University. He works near this little place.'

She pointed to a small dot on the map marked Naboomspruit.

'How do you know he's still there? That was ages ago that your sister was at university. She's been married for eight years.'

'Well, we still exchange Christmas letters,' said Marion, trying to sound as though it was the most natural thing in the world to be in contact with one's sister's old boyfriend years later. 'He was nice – a real macho Boer...'

I wasn't going to rise to that bait. Marion thought the same as I did about South Africans. I did in fact recall hearing about Jan, and I remember hoping I'd never meet him. Until now it hadn't seemed likely.

'I don't think we've got time to make any deviations.'

'Rubbish!' said Marion. 'We've got ten days before the meeting in Johannesburg. It's supposed to be a very nice nature reserve he's working at.'

This last was obviously meant to be a slight concession.

'I shan't look forward to it,' I said.

'You'll love it,' said Marion, in a tone that brooked no further discussion.

_ 17 _

Next morning we awoke early in the campsite, keen to get moving. However, we were arrested briefly by a most beautiful scene – spirals of mist arising from the marshland just in front of where we had camped, with surreal reflections of the ghostly scene in the water. Yet again I marvelled at the beauty that could be found in wild Africa, though Marion seemed keener to get breakfast under way.

Then we were on the road yet again. We drove back to Francistown, and the following day south to Palapye and across the border at Martin's Drift, with its narrow bridge spanning the broad Limpopo River. At that spot it was not so much the great, grey-green, greasy river that Rudyard Kipling had called it – rather more brown, dried-up and sandy.

Late in the afternoon we reached a gap in a game fence that announced itself as Nylsvley Natuurreservaat. We drove up a sandy track to the reserve office, which was nestled among a number of pretty rondavels – little round huts painted white, with dark, neatly thatched roofs. However, in the office we were told that Jan du Toit was actually living on the nearby farm of Buffelsvlakte.

As we drove up to the farmhouse I could see a broad figure seated in an easy chair on the front decking of the house, a can of beer beside him.

'Working hard like you did at university?' called Marion as she stopped the car.

There was a moment's silence while Jan came to terms with this unexpectedly rude intrusion; then he realised who it was.

'Ag, Marion! What a great surprise to see you again! You've finally seen the light and migrated to South Africa, hey?'

He hugged her with surprising affection. She almost disappeared in the enveloping embrace.

'This is my friend Nicholas.'

'How are you, man? Welcome!'

I found my hand trapped in a crusher.

'Hey, Sannie, come here! I told you we chose the right night for the braai.'

A figure appeared from inside and was introduced as Jan's wife Sannie. She appeared to take such arrivals in her stride.

'We ran over a warthog a few days ago,' said Jan. 'We're having a braaivleis tonight – a barbecue, you'd call it. It should be just perfect today. It's a rare treat, hey? They're protected species now – we can't shoot them. You can only eat them if you kill them by accident. Fortunately we're all crazy drivers round here.'

'There's a room for you down the corridor on the left,' said Sannie. 'I'll give you some sheets just now.'

'Are you sure this is all right?' asked Marion. 'I mean we've landed on you completely without warning.'

'Ag, man,' said Jan. 'We're a blerry sight more comfortable than the Naboom Hotel, I can tell you. Anyway, we've got a lot of news to catch up on. You must tell me what Moira is doing these days. And you yourself of course,' he added politely.

We settled into the room that Sannie showed us to, which was simple but comfortable. Sannie appeared a moment later with sheets, and left us to put them on the bed.

'Just come out to the stoep when you're ready, won't you?' Unexpected visitors were obviously no problem.

Freshened up, we went back outside and joined Jan. Sannie must have been working in the kitchen. Cans of beer were passed around and news was exchanged, mostly involving Marion and Jan. I sat back and watched and listened. I decided I could probably cope with Jan after all, at least in small doses. The bluntness was maybe not so much aggression as the result of living in the bush for many years – I'd met white Kenyan farmers too who'd lacked any social graces.

The conversation turned to our present visit, and we asked Jan if he'd ever been to the eastern part of Swaziland, especially Siteki. He said he only knew the north-western part where asbestos and iron ore were mined, but he thought his field assistant had worked in the east. He hailed a passing African farm worker.

'Hey, Philemon! You going to the compound?'

'Ja, baas.'

'You tell that lazy Moses to get himself off his woman and come up here. There's some visitors come specially from England to meet him.'

'Yebo!' The man was grinning broadly as he walked off.

Ten minutes later a tall, thin African appeared and was introduced as Moses. Jan waved him into a chair with them and handed him a can of beer. Seeing Marion's look of surprise he said:

'Something wrong?'

'Well, no, it's just that I had an idea that multiracial drinking was illegal in South Africa? Not that you always worried about legality in the past...'

Jan turned to me with an exaggerated expression of pain. 'Ag, you Engelse certainly know how hurt a guy! Now do I look like a person who would ever break the law?'

He turned back to Marion. 'The laws of this country, in their wisdom and justice, say that a Bantu gentleman may drink with white people as long as he brings his own drink. We are not allowed to offer him ours.'

He stopped to let Marion feed him with the obvious question.

'So you're telling me that Moses brought that can he's drinking?'

'Of course he did,' said Jan triumphantly. 'He brought

the whole twelve dozen cans in the house. You don't think I'm going to waste my precious time going to the bottle store, do you?'

Moses was having trouble keeping a straight face. 'Is true, missus, I do all the work around here,' he said modestly.

They were evidently a well-practised duo.

'Now,' said Jan. 'This boss wants to ask you about Swaziland. Didn't you work there in the days before you became so lazy?'

'Ja, baas, I was doing some labouring there,' replied Moses.

'Did you ever work at Siteki?' I asked.

'I work at Mpaka Mine, baas, is not far from Siteki. Sometimes we go to Siteki.'

'You never had anything to do with a firm called the Swaziland Import Export Company?'

'Hau! No, baas, these are bad people. My friend Petrus work for them once, but they sack him. They call him a thieving kaffir and throw him out and not pay him for one week. Nobody like that company.'

'D'you know what sort of work they did in that company?'

'Sorry, baas, I don't know.'

'Where is your friend Petrus now?'

'He work now in Manzini. He have a stall in handcraft market. He sell baskets to white visitors and now he have lots of money.'

The souvenir business is definitely the one to be in, I thought.

'Do you think he would still be there now if we visited the market?'

'Ja, baas, I think it. You ask for Petrus Nhlangano. You tell him you talk to me and he will help you. You tell him I come to see him soon when white boss stop making me work like slave and give me some money.'

'Hah!' said Jan. 'I give you some money when you do some work. Now, you'd better go back home. The boss has got some work to do with the braaivleis. Here, you can take this.' He passed another can of beer to Moses. 'In case you meet jackals or something on the way, you can throw it at them.'

Moses grinned. 'Dankie, m'baas. Goodbye baas, goodbye missus. I hope you like to visit Swaziland.'

'Ag, these boys are getting altogether too cheeky these days,' observed Jan as the tall figure loped off down the path, but he didn't sound too concerned about it. 'Now, I'd better go and stoke up the braai. It should be nearly ready now. Perhaps you'd like to go and see Sannie's zoo. I think she's going to feed them now.'

Sannie's zoo turned out to be a number of orphaned animals that she or Jan had found in the bush or along roads. As they entered the enclosure at the back of the house a young impala came bounding over, then recoiled a little as it saw the strangers. Not so some of the other residents. Three little furry forms raced up squeaking madly, ran over everyone's shoes, and one ran up my trouser leg. When Sannie put their food down they resolved themselves into three young banded mongooses. The food vanished as if sucked up by powerful vacuum cleaners, and two of the little animals withdrew to lick themselves. The smallest, however, sat up on its haunches and started squeaking at Sannie again.

'He likes a little cuddle,' said Sannie, and picking him up she put him down the top of her loose shift, holding her middle so that he didn't fall right down. After a brief convulsion a tiny face popped up between her breasts and peered over the edge of the dress, twittering contentedly. It stayed there while they went to look at the other animals, the prize among which was a young pangolin, or scaly anteater.

'He doesn't come from round here,' said Sannie. 'They only live in the drier parts further west. He was tiny when he walked into the house of friends of ours near Ellisras, and he wouldn't leave again. We'll have to take him back there soon and release him. He's tunnelled his way out of the enclosure twice, and he can look after himself now, but if we let him go here he'll never find a mate.'

That finished the tour. The little mongoose was removed, not without difficulty, from its mammary emplacement, and we went back to the house. I was deputed to help Jan, who was standing beside a blazing fire turning a large chunk of warthog on a spit.

'One of the secrets of a good braaivleis is to build up plenty of coals before you start,' shouted Jan above the crackling and spitting. 'Cook it long and slow, and then crisp it up at the end. Looks good, hey?'

It would have been churlish to mention that I'd once

eaten warthog in Kenya and found it like very bland pork.

'It's good that you came along,' continued Jan. 'I was going to braai the animal whole on this spit and invite the neighbours. Make a party of it. But most of the neighbours here don't like me. They call me a kaffirboetie. You know what that is? It means a native's brother. It's like in America when they call you a nigger-lover. So I thought, why waste good meat on those verkramptes? We gave half the carcase to the boys and we're having the other half.'

Salad appeared when the braai was ready, and a pot of what Sannie said was mieliepap – a thick white stodge of maize porridge served with tomato and onion gravy, probably to try to make it palatable. I had memories of a similar maize dish in Kenya, and the gravy there didn't help all that much.

And Sannie had opened a bottle of Groot Constantia Pinotage from the Cape. The wine was excellent, but all was eclipsed by the star attraction of the evening – crisp warthog, self-service from the spit. Succulent and delicious, the memory of it lingered into the night. As did the mieliepap, lying like an indigestible lead weight in the stomach...

_ 18 _

In the morning we bade our farewells. Yet again I was finding myself confused by my reactions to this country. Part of me said I should disapprove of these people and their privileged lifestyle, but another reminded me that my own was equally privileged. Jan was the baas around here, but his exchanges with Moses the evening before were hardly a typical master-servant relationship. And I'd met many white British liberals who were unable to have such spontaneous contact with black people. Maybe I'd better settle for disapproving of the neighbours. If they think Jan is a kaffirboetie they must be quite something.

We continued across the Transvaal, entered Swaziland at the Ngwenya border post, and booked in at a pleasant motel perched on a hillside just below the capital, Mbabane. With a white manager and liveried African staff it all seemed very western, and I felt more as though I was in the South Africa that I'd expected than in an independent African country. Yet another confusing contradiction.

Most of the other guests were white, and most of the

cars bore South African number plates. The only surprising feature, seen in the dining room that evening, was a formal group of Chinese dressed in Mao-style suits buttoned to their necks, sitting stiffly at their table, unsmiling and scarcely even talking. Marion discovered from one of the waiters that they were a delegation visiting a Chinese model farm set up down the road to help develop Swaziland's agriculture. I wondered how they and the exuberant Africans got on together. It must have been agony for someone. Probably both.

The next day was Sunday, and as the handcraft market at Manzini was not open we decided to have a look at Siteki. We drove down into the Ezulwini valley, through plantations of pineapple and sugarcane flanked on either side by rugged mountains, past vivid bushes of bougainvillea and poinsettia, and into the drier country beyond Manzini. Finally we began to climb into the Lubombo Mountains, and reached the little town of Siteki.

There was nobody much around to give directions, but we found the Swaziland Import-Export Co. just out of Siteki on the road to Mozambique. It was surrounded by a perimeter wire fence but the gates were open, and after watching for a while and deciding there was nobody in occupation we drove in.

The building was a newish, rectangular warehouse, fairly large and of very plain construction. The front double doors were well secured with bolts and new padlocks. We wandered around the building but it was yielding no secrets. There was a back door but it was locked, and the small windows were too high to see through. There were no incriminating coffee beans spilled on the ground near front or back doors, and no garbage bin that might have contained interesting evidence. Nothing.

'This is becoming frustrating,' said Marion. 'Real life isn't like books. In a good book there'd have been at least one clue here.'

'Let's hope Petrus can do better,' said Nicholas.

We drove back to Siteki, and noticing the petrol was low we decided to fill up if anywhere was open. We found an Esso station that didn't seem to have anyone around, but there was at least a light truck parked beside the petrol pump so we pulled in. Nobody had appeared after a couple of minutes so I wandered over to the office. The door was open so I went in.

Two black men were at the desk, one signing what looked like a petrol purchase order. As the man turned he suddenly said: 'Haugh...!', and I found myself once more staring at Peter Motokwe.

I couldn't think of anything to say so I said nothing – probably the best response in the circumstances.

Motokwe continued staring at me as he went out, and he didn't look friendly. The other black man put the papers in the till, and I said: 'Are you open for petrol?'

My heart was still thumping uncomfortably.

'Yeh, boss.' Even here I was a boss.

When I went outside with the garage man the truck had gone.

I said to Marion: 'Did you see who was inside the garage?'

'Only too well.' She looked as happy about it as Motokwe had done. 'Now we've really blown it.'

'We could have just been coming in from a visit to Mozambique,' I said hopefully.

'Pigs might fly, too. He's going to see fresh tyre marks around the shed and know we've been snooping. There weren't any when we arrived there. I noticed.'

'Shit. What do we do now?'

'What we've been doing all along the way,' replied Marion in a savage tone. 'Keep going, and let's bloody well try to think of some way to do a better job.'

She wasn't one to accept getting the worst of things.

_ 19 _

Peter Motokwe drove straight up the road to the warehouse, and peered around the main door and the compound. Then he let himself into the office, and made a quick phone call to Manzini. He made himself some coffee while he waited. Instant coffee – it was quicker and easier than the beans in the cupboard.

Nicholas and Marion registered no significance when a nondescript, light brown car pulled out from the side of the road as they approached Manzini and pottered along the road behind them. All the traffic was going that way anyway, and the bright red Mazda was easy to follow from well back. The brown car continued on to Mbabane as the red Mazda turned into a driveway conspicuously labelled as the Mdzimba Hills Motel.

Soon afterwards Peter Motokwe received a phone call from a public box outside the Mbabane General Post Office. He locked up the office again, and went to pay a call on a friend back at the Mpaka mine.

_ 20 _

That evening we decided to cheer ourselves up with a curry dinner, having seen an Indian restaurant when we first drove through Mbabane. We were already suffering withdrawal symptoms. However, the curries were terrible and the accompaniments sparse and indifferent. Maybe Sunday was a bad night, but everything tasted very old and we both felt queasy afterwards.

It struck Marion just before midnight, and she began a regular oscillation between bed and lavatory. I wasn't suffering yet, but kept half-waking as she got up. However, at half past two she woke me properly.

'I was lying in bed wondering whether sleep would come before the next dose of the runs when I heard a sort of slithering noise outside, like an animal moving around. I was half dozing and I thought that a hyena or a honey badger or something was moving outside the tent.

'Then I heard a metallic clunk and I remembered we aren't camping. After a bit I thought that maybe someone was trying to steal the car so I got up and went to the window.

I couldn't see anything, but I think we ought to take a look.'

'Good idea. You stay by the phone to call for help if anything happens to me. I'll go and have a look.'

I picked up our torch, went outside and looked all around the car. There was nobody there, and no sign that anyone might have been trying to force the door locks. I checked that they were all properly locked, then went back in.

In the morning we discussed the event as we had breakfast. A very light one since I was now suffering internal problems as well.

'It occurred to me that someone might have been trying to sabotage the car instead of stealing it. Like cutting through the brake cable or something. I don't know how they'd know where we were staying, but Peter Motokwe might have noted our number plate and they could have found us that way.'

'There's not that many flaming red Mazdas around anyway,' observed Marion sourly.

After the meal we had a careful look all over the car, but there seemed to be nothing wrong. Marion drove the car forward and hit the brakes several times, and they worked perfectly. I inspected the ground under the car carefully and found no metal filings on the ground such as a hacksaw might have produced when cutting metal cables. I looked under the side at what was visible of the brake cable and could see nothing wrong.

I still felt a bit uneasy given the target we'd been making of ourselves recently, but there wasn't much we could do about it except be vigilant. We decided our next appointment in Swaziland had to be with Petrus Nhlangano, who used to work for the Swaziland Import-Export Co., so we set off down the road towards the handcraft market at Manzini.

Shortly after we'd started I had a thought.

'The handcraft market's not going to be open if we go straight down now. Why don't we deviate along this road here?' I pointed at the map. 'It comes back out on the main road just before Manzini. The guide book says it goes up through the mountains and is very picturesque.'

Marion looked at her watch.

'Fair enough. Why's it called the Tea Road?'

'No idea. The book doesn't tell you that, of course. I've never heard of tea growing in Swaziland, but let's go and see.'

So a little further on we turned left along a gravel road. It crossed a short, flat plain, then snaked spectacularly up a steep hillside increasingly strewn with enormous boulders, up to the size of a small house. It looked as though giants had abandoned an exciting game of marbles there. No obvious tea, though.

The road continued to rise and fall like a switchback, with spectacular views at intervals across each valley. However, the lurching and bumping was too much for Marion's intestinal fortitude. As we reached the top of one of the long hauls, she pulled the car to the edge of the road and shot off towards a boulder calling:

'When you gotta go you gotta go. I'll torch that bloody

Indian restaurant when we get back to Mbabane!'

I climbed out and headed towards a boulder on the other side of the road.

'I'll come and hold the matches for you when you do it. It's got me now as well.'

I was engaged in the best relief since Mafeking when there was a loud 'whump' from the road, followed by a roaring sound.

Neither of us was in a position to rush out straight away, and when we did we saw the rear end of the car engulfed in flame which was rapidly spreading to the rest of the vehicle. We both rushed over, but there was absolutely no hope of putting the flames out.

'Jesus Christ!' said Marion. She was looking even whiter than she had from the enteritis. 'What the hell happened?'

'Cracked the petrol tank with a rock?' I said doubtfully. 'Petrol could have got on to the hot exhaust pipe.'

'I didn't hit any rocks. I was driving, remember.'

'Anyway, I don't think it would have exploded quite as sharply as that from a petrol leak. It definitely sounded like an explosion to me.'

We stared at each other as an awful possibility dawned on us.

'Peter Motokwe!' said Marion. 'Don't you remember Jerry told us in Kenya that Motokwe was once a powder boy in the mines. Used to handling explosives...'

'But how could he have got it to explode out here?'

'I don't know – I'm no expert on explosives. But how

about some sort of timing device that starts when the car is started up, or something like that, and has a time delay. He could have been fitting it when we heard the noises last night. You wouldn't want anything to go off outside the motel door – there'd be too much of an investigation then. But if it happens further away – well, the petrol tank could have cracked open on a rock...'

By this stage the car was a burning shell. There had still been a lot of petrol in the tank.

'What are we going to do now?' asked Marion.

'We'd better walk back down to the main road. We'll have to report it to the police and Avis. I can't see any point in either of us staying here. There's nothing to save, and not much anyone can do to that now.'

'We'd better be careful what we say, too. No mention of possible sabotage. Let them make their own investigation if they want to. We could wreck things if we make any comments at this stage, just when we might be getting somewhere.'

'I agree. We must have cracked the tank on a rock as we pulled over, mustn't we?'

I broke off, listening.

'Can you hear something?'

It was the sound of a motor, but it was a long way off because it took an age to reach us, getting louder and deeper all the time.

Eventually we saw an elderly African bus grinding up the hill towards us. Boxes, suitcases and a chicken coop on the roof rack, and black faces peering out of the windows as they spotted us.

The bus stopped level with us, and I read on the side that it was Mathebula's Bus & Coach Service No.1. The number was painted on the side, and it wasn't immediately clear whether this was vehicle No.1 of a great Mathebula fleet, or whether No.1 was the quality of service to be expected from Mathebula's.

The entire population of the bus evacuated itself and stood around the smouldering wreck, looking with interest and admiration.

'Haugh!' said one. 'The boss has had an accident.'

'Haugh!' said all the others.

The bus driver was a bit more practical. He offered to take us in the bus to Manzini where he was headed, which certainly beat walking back down the hot and dusty road. He refused payment even though we offered it.

We were lucky that we could offer payment. Most of our gear was back in the motel and there was hardly anything but road maps in the car. Marion had taken her handbag, containing money, passport and other papers, behind the rock with her because it also had her supply of paper tissues, and I had my valuables in a money belt.

In Manzini we reported the misfortune to the police. They rang the Avis office in Mbabane, then drove us back out in a police Land Rover for an on-the-spot inspection. Then back to Manzini where laborious statements were taken and typed. Finally we were released, transportless, but at least the police hadn't thought there was anything suspicious. Maybe vehicles burst into flames all the time in Swaziland. They certainly hadn't shown much curiosity.

We rang the Avis receptionist who'd meanwhile checked the insurance situation with headquarters in Johannesburg. We'd opted for full cover having heard about high accident rates in southern Africa, and Avis promised to replace the car immediately. They had one in Mbabane but no spare driver to bring it down to Manzini, so we agreed to come up on the bus. Mathebula's, of course.

At the bus terminus we found there wasn't a bus for another hour and a half, so we wandered into the handcraft market to look for Petrus.

Petrus Nhlangano was clearly doing well in the souvenir handicraft business. He was dressed in a dark suit that exuded prosperity, and was quite fat. I passed on the greeting and introduction from Moses, which evidently amused him, and then said:

'We just wanted to ask you something about the Swaziland Import Export Company at Siteki. Moses told us you worked there once.'

'Ah, yes, I worked there once but they gave me the sack, you know.'

Petrus spoke excellent English and was obviously used to dealing with Europeans. The absence of 'boss' from his conversation was refreshing.

'It is a bad company.'

'Er, yes, that was what we wanted to talk to you about. We

believe they're doing some bad things concerning ivory...?'

I left it hanging in the hope that he would know something, and he did.

He laughed. 'Ha! yes, the coffee shipments, you mean?'

'Exactly. The pieces of tusk come in the bottom wrapped in plastic bags, don't they?'

'Ja, I used to work on that. We would shovel the coffee out of the top into empty boxes, and label them to go to Johannesburg. Then we took out some packets of plastic foam...'

Marion shot me a triumphant glance at that.

'...and then there were the tusks at the bottom, just in one layer, you know. We put them all into one box and sealed it. We painted out the name from Kenya on the side, and put our name on it. Then the boss would do some papers for it and a man would drive it to Botswana. That is all we did, you know.'

'Do you remember the name of the place in Kenya that you had to paint over?'

'Ha! now, I can't remember that, you know!' He thought for a minute. 'No, it was a long time ago for me. But my friend Lazarus, he still works there. I will ask him and you can come back to see me again.'

'That would be great. Would it be too soon if we came back tomorrow?'

'No, I think that is okay. Now, would you perhaps need any baskets while you are here? These ones are very cheap and I can give you fifty per cent discount on these...'

He wasn't going to miss an opportunity, and he launched into an impressively fluent sales pitch. We didn't want to do anything that would diminish his willingness to see Lazarus for us, so we bought a small basket, a wooden carving, and a thing looking like a woven straw sock that Petrus assured us was a traditional strainer for the thick native Swazi beer. Fortunately we could hide the last two in the basket before we got on to the bus.

In Mbabane we had to fill in a further detailed statement for Avis's insurance claim, and then a new contract to hire the replacement car. This was a Volkswagen beetle since there were no Mazdas to spare. At the motel we decided to leave it in the general parking area so it couldn't be identified as ours. We were slowly learning to be more careful.

We sat down that evening to a light fish dinner in the motel dining room – the nearest thing to invalid food we could think of. The traumas of the day had caught up with the curry of the night before, and we sat in rather numb silence.

Finally Marion said:

'I was just thinking about the car going up like that today. I've been having nightmares all day about what we'd look like now if we'd been inside it, but it also occurred to me that if we'd gone with it nobody would know anything about the way the ivory's getting out of Kenya. All our discoveries would be wasted, and Pendleton would still be safe. I'd go to my grave easier if I knew I was taking him along with me.'

'You're right, we should let somebody know about it. I wonder who'd be best?'

'Why not Peter Marston? He knows a lot of the background already. We could send him the details and ask him to hang on to them, but if anything happens to us to pass them on to Ezekiel. Or to Malcolm Gibson at a pinch. That way it wouldn't be lost like Fergus's information was.'

So after dinner Marion wrote out a précis of our findings. The trail of ivory from a Kenya coffee business to Swaziland, how it was repackaged and shipped to Botswana, and the additional evidence that Huntsman Safaris must be deeply involved because of the observed activities of Peter Motokwe.

I added a note about our suspicions over the combustion of the car, and we left a space for the insertion of a Kenyan name, in the hope that Petrus would be able to tell us something tomorrow.

Hopefully it would all help to scupper the ivory smuggling, but it didn't get anyone any nearer to proving that Pendleton killed Fergus Campbell.

That night our sleep was interrupted by nothing more than me disposing at intervals of my fish dinner. I shouldn't have been so stupid as to eat it.

When we went outside next morning, the air was full of smoke from grass fires that had been burning on the hillsides during the night. It was an unwelcome reminder of what had happened to us the day before, and it left the atmosphere thick and stuffy. We packed the car, checked out of the motel and drove down to Manzini.

'Let's hope Petrus has been able to find out something.

I'm getting rather sick of Swaziland,' said Marion.

Petrus had. We found him in a cafe near the market, and he passed us a slip of paper on which was written RUIRU HIGHLAND PLANTATIONS KENYA.

We thanked him profusely and made to leave, but Petrus had not earned his fortune as a trader through missing opportunities. He took me by the arm and guided me back to the market to see some new stock that had just arrived, the like of which we would see nowhere else in Africa, he assured us.

As a gesture of goodwill we bought a set of rush tablemats and two seed necklaces. We were glad we could point to the cramped Beetle as a reason for refusing a rushwork laundry bin shaped like an amphora, which was supposedly one of the greatest bargains in Swaziland at the time. It would have fitted into the Mazda.

We inserted the Kenyan name in the letter to Peter Marston and posted it at Manzini post office. Then with sighs of relief we drove off up the road and back to the city of Johannesburg.

_ 21 _

We arrived in the Golden City, and made our way to the Hotel Egoli. This required a series of devious manoeuvres among one-way streets that all seemed to go the wrong way. The hotel was the latest addition to Johannesburg's range of five-star palaces, complete with obligatory African commissionaire in top hat and morning dress uniform, like a performer from a black-and-white minstrel show.

It was here that the Biological Society of Southern Africa was due to assemble in two days' time for its meeting. However, when we discovered how much the rooms were, we moved on to the less pretentious suburb of Hillbrow. It wasn't so much that we couldn't have afforded it for a few days, but I've never liked paying for a lot of services that I don't want and won't use.

Next day we wandered around the city shopping centre, looking at the sumptuous displays of consumer goods and gifts. It did appear that the sale of ivory was much restricted because we saw very little on offer, but the arrays of gemstones and gold and silver ornaments were breathtaking in their beauty and richness.

Outside on the pavements legless and deformed beggars slid across the kerbstones towards us, hands outstretched and saying 'Pliss, pliss!' This came out mainly as a hiss, which heightened the gruesome contrast between the poverty outside and the bland opulence inside.

It occurred to me that one of the tiny, exquisite gold pendants was probably months of salary for even a better-paid African, let alone the one who was sweeping the jeweller's floor. Once again the huge contrasts of this country were making me uncomfortable. In Britain I would simply have delighted in the beauty of the jeweller's creations, but here it just seemed obscene.

The following day we went to the zoo, but this was also no pleasure. Many of the animals were confined in conditions under which they couldn't lead a normal life, and the ones that could were stuck away in distant homelands at the back of the zoo that nobody went to look at.

Then at last it was time for the meeting. We returned our car to Avis and settled the account for it and the defunct Mazda, then went to the Hotel Egoli and booked in at the conference reception.

The Biological Society of Southern Africa had negotiated a bargain deal with the hotel, to judge by what Peter Marston had paid and what the reception had wanted to charge us two days earlier. We introduced ourselves to the conference organiser, Dirk Pienaar, who smiled at us with harassed vagueness, pressed a room key in our hands, and tried to answer two telephones at once. We decided it would be tactful to wait a little before bothering him about where we might find Professor Carpenter.

The first item on the conference programme was an informal cocktail party. Dirk Pienaar was obviously experienced enough to know that the first thing people want to do at such gatherings is renew old acquaintances, and a formal session is generally boycotted in favour of the bar.

We each took a glass of Cape white wine and wandered round the room, but we didn't find anyone we knew. The people were the typical mixture of a biological meeting, a few normal, many clearly eccentric. A few were elegantly over-dressed, while others looked as though they had spent the last six months looking for Dr Livingstone in deepest Africa, or sleeping on park benches.

An old woman and an old man exchanged boxes of pinned insects, then rapidly turned aside and peered at each other's gifts through tiny hand lenses like children scrutinising presents at a birthday party. An elderly woman was displaying dried grasses immaculately laid out in herbarium sheets. A small bald man fanned what looked like a hand of large playing cards and pointed to the different spots on each. They turned out to be rodent skins stretched tight over pieces of card, and he was showing the different markings.

Further collecting trips were also under way as guests regularly passed the bar, collecting liquid specimens as they went. The noise level rose rapidly, and neither of us noticed

Dirk Pienaar at Marion's elbow.

'I'm terribly sorry, when you introduced yourself just now it never occurred to me. Are you the Dr MacTaggart who's been working on raptors in East Africa?'

'Yes, I am.' Marion looked mildly surprised that her fame had spread this far, though the surprise would have been mild.

'Oh, marvellous! I've been reading your recent papers in the International Journal of Avian Ecology. I have a student who's just starting work in the Kruger Park on the ecology of the martial eagle. He's here at the meeting and I'd be most grateful if you'd let him have a chat with you, to pick up some practical tips.'

'I'd be delighted,' said Marion, 'but I'm a bit out of practice with big birds. I'm studying English hawks these days, which is a rather different league.'

I thought again of the martial eagles I'd seen in East Africa when Marion had been working on them. Fiercely majestic birds dwarfing the branches on which they perched, their handsome white fronts speckled like a nobleman's ermine.

'I'm sure you don't forget something like that. Please let me take you over and introduce you to him.' He sounded desperate to have someone help the student, and Marion could never resist anything like that. Anyone who studied big raptors had to be a top person.

Dirk made the introductions, and he was just turning away when I thought this was my moment.

'Can I just ask you something for a moment. Marion

and I are very keen to meet Professor Carpenter while we're here. I wonder if you could point him out to me?'

'I'm afraid he hasn't arrived yet. He's only just finished some work in South America. He's coming over on the direct flight from Rio, but his plane was delayed by a technical fault. He's actually due to land about now. My assistant's just gone to Jan Smuts to meet him.'

Yet another delay, but hopefully Carpenter would be here soon. I stood listening to Marion holding forth to the student about techniques for gaining access to eagles' nests without losing one's eyes, scalps or other parts of the anatomy. It was a far cry from my penduline tits. The aggrieved parents just twittered furiously at me when I had to disturb their nests.

The cocktail party broke up as an early evening meal was announced, after which the delegates, comfortably replete with food and alcohol, sat back or dozed in anticipation of the formal opening.

The meeting opened with a speech of welcome from no less than a government minister, delivered in thickly accented and halting English, with occasional fragments of Afrikaans. It was followed by a business meeting consisting of endless circular discussion of proposed changes to the Society's constitution.

My attention quickly wandered, and I looked again for possible signs of Professor Carpenter. I hadn't noticed any new arrivals other than the minister, and there were no obvious Americans in attendance. Given our bad luck to date, I was really worried that something would prevent

Carpenter coming at the last moment.

But next morning my fears were eased. Dirk Pienaar entered escorting a short, upright, sprightly man, with a West Point haircut and wearing a bright blue tuxedo-style jacket, medium pink shirt and spotted bow tie, tapered grey flannel trousers, and tan shoes. A snappy dresser....

Marion gave me a look of triumphant glee as the guest mounted the podium and was introduced to the assembly as Professor Byron Carpenter. His address was to conclude the entire meeting, presumably so as not to put too many of the other speakers in the shade.

Then the scientific sessions started. The first speaker gave an account of the microfauna of accumulations of bat droppings in deep caves in the Transvaal. It had a certain amount of interest but was accompanied by far too many flashlight pictures of piles of bat guano. I heard one man near me say quite loudly: 'Ag, come on, man, one heap of bat shit looks like all the others!' This use of 'man' by South Africans was beginning to amuse me, especially since in this case the lecture was being given by a woman.

The second speaker was no improvement. A thin man of unbelievable antiquity and slowness, he recounted in a piping monotone the history of a plant-recording scheme in the Cape Province, illustrated with slides of tables from a book that contained so much detail that even the front row must have had trouble reading them. At times he stopped altogether, as though his power supply had inadvertently been switched off.

Morning coffee came as a great relief, and thank God the subsequent talks weren't as bad. One fluent and enthusiastic young woman held the room in fascinated silence as she described a scheme of 'restaurants' for vultures to prevent their extinction in semi-wild areas. In regions like the Magaliesberg, a line of mountains running westwards from Pretoria, the Cape vulture that once flourished there was dying. There was too little unfarmed land left to support the population of game animals whose carrion the vultures used to eat, and the farmers always buried carcases when their own stock died.

The vultures were reduced to scavenging at rubbish tips, but this diet didn't contain enough bones and their young suffered from calcium deficiency. The nestlings lay on the rock-ledge nests with deformed legs and wings, and if they got as far as attempting to fly they plummeted down the ravine to a splattered death below. It was a sad case of magnificent creatures being unable to adapt to conditions changed by humans.

So a group of volunteers had established a scheme whereby sympathetic farmers notified them of available carcases, and they carted these to places in the mountains where the vultures would find and feed on them. The birds had come to know the signs, and the helpers would see them circling before the truck had even disgorged its load. Last year, for the first time in many years, the chick from each of the known nests had fledged successfully.

It was a positive and encouraging study, but you couldn't

please everyone.

'My family owns a sheep farm,' said one man standing up, pink in the face. 'These vultures attack our sheep, they kill the lambs. They are vermin. They should be killed, not encouraged!'

The young woman who had presented the paper was clearly well used to this line of attack. 'Sir, your statement is based on a misconception that vultures are predators. They aren't. They're carrion feeders, that wait for something else to kill the animals first. Maybe it is jackals that are killing your lambs, or a hyena. The vultures do the cleaning up for you.'

The pink face rose out of the audience again, but the chairman saw it coming. He knew an endless debate when he saw one.

'Thank you, ladies and gentlemen. This has been a most interesting paper and discussion. I see that lunch is now ready, and so that we can make a prompt start at two o'clock I suggest we all go to eat now.'

He sat down again, probably hoping that lunch was indeed ready.

After lunch we managed to corner Professor Carpenter. We introduced ourselves as East African ornithologists and asked if we could hear sometime about his experiences in Amboseli.

'You're very welcome,' he replied in a broad drawl. 'My, that was a fascinating place. I sure hope I get back there real soon. Say, I guess we're about to start again, but how about you come up to my suite after dinner tonight and have a drink then. About half after eight?'

I started to say that that would be great, but I was drowned out by a bell announcing the start of the next session. Carpenter gave us a cheery wave and returned to his reserved seat at the front. He hadn't sounded at all reluctant to talk about Amboseli.

We sat through an afternoon of such diverse topics as strategies of drought resistance by savanna trees, the development of the reproductive organs of the elephant (some amazing slides there), shark attacks at Natal coastal resorts (gruesome slides this time), and the diatoms of Table Bay. But I was thinking of Amboseli and Professor Carpenter.

_ 22 _

After dinner we took the lift up to Professor Carpenter's top floor suite with keen anticipation. We took with us a bottle of Theuniskraal Gewürztraminer as a goodwill offering. It came from the Tulbagh area of the Cape, and the barman told us it would be a pleasant after-dinner wine. Which indeed it was, but Professor Carpenter preferred to stick to bourbon on the rocks, which he'd laid on with ready accessibility.

'Now tell me, you're both working in Amboseli at the moment?'

'No, we were until last year,' replied Marion. 'In Amboseli and Masai Mara, but our grants finished, unfortunately. We're working in Britain at the moment, and wondering how we might get back to East Africa.'

'Yeah, well, I don't blame you for that. I was *most* impressed with it while I was there, and I'm planning to spend more time there as soon as I can. Now, Dr MacTaggart, you were working on eagles there, were you not?'

'Yes. And please call me Marion – it's much easier!'

'Yeah, I remember reading your papers. Most interesting, and so nice to have a comparative study of several species. Most people just look at one species. And Dr Twistleton? I mean, er, Nicholas...?'

'I was studying the penduline tits. I have a couple of papers in press in Ornithologia at the moment.'

I was determined to stick up for tits, which had been getting short shrift at the conference so far.

'Sure, they were excellent papers!'

'They haven't been published yet,' I said.

I was beginning to wonder how trustworthy were any comments that he made.

'I guess that's right, but the journal just happened to send them to me as a referee.' He grinned. 'Passed with no problems. It was nice to find someone who could still write good English.'

Carpenter was forgiven, and my tits were vindicated.

'The thing that impressed me most about Amboseli,' continued Carpenter, 'was how accessible the birds were. You may know I go in a lot for bird photography – it's a kinda hobby as well as work. I've done a lot in the rainforests of Central and South America. You have to make clearings, set up lures, go to all sorts of trouble just to get one good shot, but in Africa, well, they just sit there on the bushes and let you zoom in on them. I got some fantastic shots, and I blasted off so much film I had the FBI call on me when I got home. I guess they musta thought I'd been buying blue movies!'

Marion looked at me with raised eyebrows, and I nodded.

'We can actually tell you why the FBI called on you, as it happens.'

It was Carpenter's turn then to raise his eyebrows, high.

'It was quite coincidental that it was you. But before we tell you, can I ask just one thing? What was your impression of Charles Pendleton who took you round? I mean, how did you actually judge him as a person?'

'Hm. Let me fix myself another shot first.'

He was obviously buying a bit of time to think, and he took a while getting the drink.

'Okay. I don't know what in hell this is leading to, but I've got nothing to hide and my instinct tells me you're straight people too. I have to say that Pendleton gave me an excellent trip. He's a very professional safari operator. We had no hitches from start to finish, he knew his African birds extremely well, and what's more he knew exactly where to go to find each one. But I guess that's not what you're after, since you asked me what I thought of him as a person.'

He paused.

'I guess we got on okay just about all of the time, but I can't say that I really liked him. You know how it is with some people, they don't do anything wrong, but your instinct still tells you to dislike them. Well, I guess it was like that with him. I felt there was something kinda hard underneath him. He knew all the birds and animals, but he didn't have the affection for them that you or I would have. I figured they were just commercial items to him, that enabled him to run his expensive safaris because they were there for him to show to people. Okay, that's my bit. Now shoot...'

'Well, you're spot on when you said he sees wildlife in commercial terms, but in a rather worse way than you guessed. Did you know he used to be a professional hunter?'

'No, he never told me. But I noticed his company was called Huntsman Safaris. I thought that was in poor taste.'

'But it's even worse than that. The Kenyan police have good evidence that he's involved in poaching ivory from the National Parks. And to complete the indictment, a police officer investigating the business was murdered in Masai Mara not long ago.'

'Okay, but what's all this got to do with me? I've never been to Masai Mara.'

He was beginning to sound a bit impatient.

'Well, the police would have good reason for suspecting Pendleton of the murder, except for the fact that you give him a perfect alibi. The murder happened while you and he were at Amboseli.'

'Jeeesus H. Christ!'

Carpenter let out a long, slow breath.

'So that's why the FBI were asking me all those weird questions. Kept wanting to know if I'd left Amboseli any time, or if Carpenter ever left me for a while. But how do you come into this? Are you working for the Kenyan police or something?'

'No, we just happened to be good friends of the police

inspector who was murdered. And we don't like ivory poachers. We went to Kenya for the summer vacation and started asking a few questions. We heard about your alibi for Pendleton, and then we had the chance of coming in someone's place to this conference where you were speaking, so we thought we'd try to talk to you. We just felt we might have more of the local background than the FBI would have had, and we might pick up something that happened while you were there that they wouldn't notice as significant.'

'You're very welcome. Jesus! If I'd known it was anything like that I'd have tried a lot harder. Fire away!'

'Well, the one thing that particularly occurred to us was that Pendleton has a plane, and he could have flown from Amboseli to Masai Mara, committed the murder and flown back again. He needn't have left you for more than about five hours, maybe even a little less. Do you remember him being away for a period like that?'

Carpenter thought for a minute or two.

'Gee, I'm sorry to disappoint you over this, but I'm sure he wasn't ever away for that sort of time. I keep a detailed diary and I can check it later. I've got it with me here somewhere because it's got all my notes on African birds. But I'm sure he never left me for as long as that. The reason I'm so positive is that it was a kinda weird trip that way. I was there six days in all, and I never saw another soul the entire time. On the other hand I was almost never free of Pendleton's company. I think he went off three or four times in total, but it was never for more than about half an hour.

Well, maybe an hour at the most. He went to collect fresh supplies.'

'When you say you never saw another soul, there must have been an African cook and servant, though?'

'No, nobody. Pendleton did all of that himself. Said he didn't think it was right for people to use menials like that.'

Marion's snort almost drowned out mine.

'Try telling that to the servants he normally has in his camp,' said Marion. 'His company's got a reputation for driving its Africans hard and not paying them much, and he's certainly got plenty in his main camp. This whole thing is very odd.'

'I thought he didn't seem all that practised at the cooking. Though I must say we ate okay while I was there.'

'So it was just the two of you in your own little camp?'

'Yeah. I don't know which part of the park it was, but it seemed to be well away from any inhabited areas. He said I'd get a better feel for the African bush that way, and it sure worked out like that. We had lions, jackals and hyenas round the tent at night, and there were birds everywhere. You shoulda heard the dawn choruses! We were right near a river so there was plenty of water, and I guess that also drew the wildlife. I loved to lie in bed and listen to the hippopotamuses barking and grunting.'

'Mm, I'd agree with you about living out in the bush. I guess I can see Pendleton's point. But I just can't understand why there wasn't at least one servant.'

'Perhaps he felt they would cause extra disturbance?'

'Well, maybe...'

Most unlikely in Pendleton's case. There was something very odd about this.

'Could you roughly describe your visit, in case there's anything else unusual about it? Right from Nairobi.'

'Sure. It all went pretty smoothly, really. I flew in from Rome. My plane was slightly early. I went through all the formalities and expected to have to wait for Pendleton, but he was already there to meet me. We loaded up my baggage and flew off in his plane soon afterwards to Amboseli.'

'But I thought you were late arriving at Amboseli?' said Marion.

Carpenter frowned at her. 'Well, I guess I did take a bit of time getting through customs with all my equipment and cameras and things. But I didn't think we were really running very late.'

He paused, but we didn't say anything so he went on.

'The trip down to Amboseli was the most superb I've ever had in a little airplane. Smooth all the way. It was early morning so the sun was still low, and the landscape was bathed in soft yellow light. The mountains were making long, sharp shadows. I've got some real good pictures of it back home. And you know how you always seem to get the sun on your lens in a small plane around sunrise. This time the sun was nearly behind us, which was great.'

Marion was frowning, but didn't say anything.

'We landed at Amboseli,' continued Carpenter. 'There was a Land Rover with a black driver there to meet us.

Pendleton took me in the wagon and left the black guy to look after the plane. I asked him later if the poor guy would still be stuck there with the plane, but he told me not to worry.'

'It all sounds quite strange and unusual to me,' I said. 'But I'm damned if I can make any sense of it.'

Carpenter raised his eyebrows.

'I just figured that was the way they organise things out here. Anyway, I had an amazing six days watching and photographing birds out in the bush, which was what I was there for. I got some of the best shots of my life. I'm going to put some of them together for National Geographic real soon. They've seen the shots and they're pretty keen. I got one shot of a Senegal coucal that must be the greatest picture I've ever taken. I'm going to put it on during my lecture. It isn't really relevant but I just have to show it! Here, lemme show you...'

He went over to an expensive-looking slide box and ran his finger down the index card.

I was experiencing a slight sense of disappointment. Even the greatest ornithologist in the world was fallible, and muddled up his coucals. Easy to do, admittedly, with coucals, but the Senegal did not occur at Amboseli – only the very similar white-browed coucal.

Carpenter brought over the slide, neatly labelled with date, locality and bird name, and we each held it up to the light and peered at it. I'd been wondering whether I could be rude enough to tell someone as eminent as Carpenter that he'd got his identification wrong, but when I saw the picture I could see why the mistake had occurred. At least without further magnification the bird did indeed look like a Senegal coucal. Perhaps it actually constituted a genuine new record for Amboseli, though one couldn't officially record it from a photo.

'It's certainly a fantastic shot – it'll be great to see it on the big screen in your lecture. Did Pendleton take you out to the Loginya swamps to see the long-toed lapwings?'

'Gee, do they have them in that park? That's a real pity, I sure would have liked some shots of them. They're a neat example of parallel evolution with the jacanas and other lily-trotters, and I'm trying to collect a variety of examples of parallel evolution. No, we didn't go to that sort of habitat.'

'That's funny! Apart from the lapwings it's a good spot for the occasional Madagascar squacco, not to mention a whole range of swamp birds. I'd have thought that would be one of the first places to take an ornithologist.'

'Ah, well, I guess I didn't have too much time there. That lapwing'll be a good excuse for going back, anyway!'

He replaced the coucal slide in the box, then rummaged in his bag.

'I said I could tell you when Pendleton was away from the camp. Lemme see...' He flipped the early pages of the book.

'I arrived on a Sunday and I left again the next Saturday. Pendleton went off late Monday afternoon, but that was only for about half an hour. I remember that because I offered to peel vegetables while he was away and…' – he had a slightly sheepish grin – '…. I hadn't finished them when he got back. I guess it's quite a few years since I did that sort of thing. I live at a campus residence, you know.

'Now, let me see, he went off again on the Wednesday and then once more on the Thursday, both times late in the afternoon, and that was it. I don't have a record of how long he was away, but I'm sure it was only about the same as the first time. No, maybe it was a bit longer on the last because that was when I got involved in taking movie film of a heron fishing beside the river and I remember the light was going fast. But he wouldn't have been more than an hour at the most. Anyway I guess you can't fly after dark in those places, so he couldn't have been up in an airplane.'

'No, I'm sure you're right,' said Marion. 'There are no lights anywhere. And that was all, was it?'

'Yeah, that was it. On the Saturday midday he drove me back to the airstrip. If you can call it that. No windsock, and it looked more like a patch of grass to me. And the same…'

I had to interrupt. 'That's another peculiar thing. The runway at Amboseli is quite well formed and there's a huge windsock standing clearly at one end.'

'Well, maybe I wasn't looking too well,' said Carpenter. 'Anyway, the same black guy was there with the plane, and we left him with the Land Rover while we flew back to Nairobi. End of trip, end of story!'

'It was very good of you to talk to us like this,' said Marion. 'I have to admit I'm more mystified than ever at the moment, but you never know. If we think about it for a while it might eventually make some sense.'

'It was my pleasure entirely. I'd certainly be happy to do whatever I can to stop ivory poaching. If you think of anything else you'd like to talk to me about, don't hesitate to ask.'

'Thank you very much, we will. Well, I guess we'd better be getting along to bed. Nicholas?'

'Yes. Thank you, Professor Carpenter. Good night.'

'Good night to you both. Pleasant dreams of Amboseli. I shall.'

Back in our room we discussed the whole business again. The whole account seemed bizarre, and for that reason quite suspicious, but whether the suspicion should fall on both Pendleton and Carpenter or just on Pendleton we couldn't decide. The only conclusion we could draw was that nothing made much sense at all.

_ 23 _

Next day was the optional excursion day, and we decided to go. The only alternative was another day drifting around Johannesburg, and anything was going to be better than that. Besides, Professor Carpenter would be on the outing and it would be a chance to see how good he was on southern African birds. Not that that was relevant to anything much, of course, but when you've run out of other ideas...

The excursion was to Suikerbosrand Nature Reserve, which turned out to be bleakly brown-grassed hills and plains near Heidelberg, just south-east of Johannesburg. The excursion notes told us that the reserve was being developed particularly as an area where cheetahs could multiply in safety, and I was looking forward to seeing this most elegant and graceful of African animals again. I thought of the times Marion and I had seen these beautiful beasts in Amboseli and Masai Mara; the essence of grace in their movements, muscles defined like an anatomist's drawing, rippling under a golden pelt elegantly spotted with black. The little cubs, too, one minute rolling around like kittens, the next standing upright on a log like a haughty beast of prey. Which they were practising to become.

Alas for memories. Cheetahs are not only beautiful but sensible, and they had the wisdom to stay well out of the way of the group of buses lumbering round the dusty tracks of the reserve. One was seen briefly, accelerating into the distance with its amazing stride and speed, but for the most part it was the usual impala and a token eland. This didn't seem to worry the party unduly because the major object of the excursion for many seemed to be the lunchtime braaivleis, sumptuously laid on by the Park staff behind the information office. Tactfully the meat was from a butcher rather than being impala or warthog or something, and it was accompanied by the inevitable huge black cooking pot of mieliepap with its bowl of gravy.

There was, however, a good variety of birds in the reserve. Not some of the more spectacular ones that prefer less open country, but there were waterholes, small swamps and lakes with waders, egrets and herons, and weaver birds darting in and out of their tight capsule nests hanging from the fringing reeds. And there were the assorted birds of African grassland, many of them camouflaged to be invisible against their background and therefore small and nondescript brown. They were among the hardest birds to identify unless you were a true expert.

Which Professor Carpenter turned out to be. We made sure we were on the same bus as he was and sitting near him, and we found we were no competition when it came to identifications. We listened in amazement as he picked bird after bird and described the habits and peculiarities of each, hesitating on only a few. It was all the more impressive if you accepted Carpenter's claim that this was the first time he'd ever visited South Africa – maybe he was actually more familiar with the countries of Africa than he was letting on. Maybe he was a regular visitor who was involved with wildlife poaching…?

That evening Marion looked distinctly gloomy.

'We just don't seem to be getting anywhere with our investigation. We're always waiting for some exciting break-through and it never happens. Why don't we just go back to Kenya, shoot Pendleton and have done with it?'

I was beginning to feel the same way. However, I thought I'd better try to keep the investigation afloat a bit longer. I had a nagging feeling that somehow the key to the whole business was lying in Carpenter's story, but I couldn't think how. It was his account of his tour with Pendleton that provided the only inconsistencies in the whole picture, but they made no sense at the moment.

'I know how you feel, but I think we should hang on for Carpenter's closing address. If we can see his slides, they just *might* crack the whole thing.'

It didn't sound convincing even to me.

* * *

The next day certainly dragged. It was a symposium presenting the results of a multidisciplinary study of the ecology of South African mopane woodland. Some of the individual papers had interest, but they were of variable quality and direction and there seemed to be little synthesis into an overall picture of the working of the ecosystem. The brightest note of the session came when we were hailed by Carpenter at the morning coffee break.

'Hey, you guys! You like Middle Eastern food? We've been told there's a really good restaurant here that serves it. A group of us are booking a table for tonight – you wanna be in on it?'

'I've hardly eaten much Middle Eastern food before...' I began.

'Yes,' said Marion.

She wasn't going to let me sabotage the chance of a good meal.

'Boy, you've got a treat in store if you don't know it,' said Carpenter. 'One of the great art forms of the world if you like eating.'

'Sounds like my style,' murmured Marion. 'We're on!'

So later that evening a group of biologists, sated with mopane and hungry for real food, filed out of the hotel and walked three blocks down the street to the modest portals of the al-Baghdadi eating house. Named according to the menu from the last part of the very long name of an early cookbook author – his manuscript had appeared in Baghdad in 1226, shortly before the city was sacked by Mongols – it made up for its external plainness by a sumptuous interior and, as it turned out, its dedication to good food.

The entire party was placed on cushions round a low, circular table, set with an array of small dishes of food laid out in a pleasing mosaic of bright and pastel colours. A tall, grinning African in a long gown – presumably meant to be a Nubian slave, but his face was probably more that of a Zulu warrior – came up to us with a bowl of scented water, and took it from person to person saying 'Wishee, washee!'. He found it all a huge joke and his gaiety was infectious, for the noise level at the table rose rapidly.

The manager came up to greet us.

'Salaam aleikum!'

'Aleikum es salaam,' replied one or two of the party who knew the ropes, or had been to the Middle East before.

'I understand that a few of you here have not tried our food before, so I will explain.' He waved at the table. 'We have put for you some appetisers to stimulate your palate, before we bring you the main food. That is hoummous, perhaps you will all know that, it is a paste made mostly from chickpeas. You scoop it up with pieces of this pitta bread. This one you scoop too, it is baba ghanoush, it is from aubergine and tahina which you call sesame seed, and some lemon. It is very good.

'These little balls are ta'amia, or in Egypt they call them falafel, they are from the powder of dried beans with spices and we fry them. This one is bamia – that is what you call okra, with tomato and onions. And these are dolmeh – they are vine leaves with savoury filling.

'Now this one is a favourite with me, it is fûl medames. It is the brown fûl bean of Egypt and we mash it with olive oil and lemon juice. Very simple, but you will find that the bean gives it a most delicious flavour. Now, you please will start to try these, and then I come to tell you about our soups!'

I gazed at the assortment of dishes, and was still wondering which to try first when I noticed that Marion already had four of them on her plate and had half demolished her first pitta eating them.

The only time I'd eaten anything vaguely Middle Eastern had been in a kebab house in England. They had served hoummous first and I'd quite liked it, so I went for that first. This version was infinitely tastier than the English one, and when I graduated to baba ghanoush I was entranced by the subtle, smoky flavour. After that I was hooked and I ate far too much of all of them. I wondered how they could be made so delicious, and I had my answer later when I realised that the one ingredient in most that the manager hadn't mentioned was garlic.

The manager returned to describe the various soups that were available. I opted out but my neighbour ordered Persian wheat soup, and Marion went for Armenian yoghurt soup, made from beaten egg and yoghurt with noodles, onion and mint. Even the sight of it made me feel fuller. I was regretting having got carried away on entrees.

Orders were then taken for main courses, but before they were served the manager came back to the table.

'I am asking for Professor Carpenter,' he said looking around at them.

Carpenter raised his hand.

'Ah, they tell me you are a great expert on birds, yes?'

'Well, I'm not sure. I still have a lot to learn.'

'Perhaps you can help me with this one!'

The manager snapped his fingers at an African waiter, who came forward with a platter on which stood a plump, roasted bird, golden brown and bulging at the seams, with two white feathers tucked facetiously into the sides.

Carpenter gave an amused snort as it was set down. He said: 'This is a bird of such rarity and beauty that a mortal like myself would not dare to name it...'

Then he looked around to see who might have set him up for that one.

'Ha, we call this Persian roast chicken,' said the manager. 'The bird is stuffed full with dried fruit and apple and cinnamon before we roast it. Is very delicious but very rich. Please to try some while you eat!'

Then the other main courses were brought out. I'd chosen fattah, a dish of lamb and aubergine pieces on a bed of toasted pitta, smothered in yoghurt with herbs and spices and evident garlic. Marion had chicken in pomegranate sauce. My other neighbour had lamb stewed with rhubarb, and we all shared around. Plates of saffron rice and several different salads were spread around, and the table looked in the end as though it would not have needed any miracle to feed the five thousand.

I managed to cope because the meal proceeded at a leisurely pace, but I felt a sense of relief when the food was eventually cleared away. This was short-lived because the dishes were replaced with trays of eastern sweetmeats, small but very rich, such as dates stuffed with almond paste, balls of rich apricot confection, variants of baklava and halva, Turkish delight, and more. The pièce de résistance was a large bowl of what the manager described as dried fruit salad: plump whole dried apricots and raisins macerated for days in rose-water and orange blossom water, with almonds, pistachios and pine nuts.

Even Marion was reduced to picking delicately at this selection, although by the time the coffee was drunk she had made a respectable hole into her section. The coffee was most refreshing for it had been cooked with cardamom, the fragrance of which soothed the palate and the digestion.

We both agreed afterwards that our repertoire of exotic food was now firmly enlarged beyond curries. That judgement was only slightly dented by the heavy indigestion we suffered throughout the night....

_ 24 _

A nd so the last day of the conference arrived. Delegates came to the meeting room in their travelling clothes, some with their suitcases ready for a sprint to the first taxi, but they were clearly not going to leave until they had heard Professor Carpenter's concluding address. Word had spread about the quality of his slides.

The first speaker of the morning described infertility problems of the white rhinoceros, and the second discussed a recent survey of plants used as medicines by the Bantu peoples of South Africa. Then after the morning coffee break Professor Byron Carpenter mounted the rostrum.

He apologised for the fact that most of his talk would be on parallel evolution among the rainforest birds of South America and South East Asia, but he had not yet been able to visit the rainforests of Africa, a deficiency he hoped soon to remedy. However, he promised to conclude with some observations on African savanna birds in relation to those he had seen in similar country in Argentina and Brazil.

He showed some beautiful slides of the often colourful

and spectacular birds of the forests, and the audience was more hushed than at any previous stage in the conference. Then he began to compare the savanna birds, and I began to feel disappointment and suspicion as one or two anomalies showed up.

The first was the slide of the coucal that we'd looked at in Carpenter's room. When projected there was no doubt that the bird had been correctly named as a Senegal coucal, for it completely lacked the white eyebrows and barred upper tail-coverts of the white browed coucal. I conceded the identification and found it an interesting new record for Amboseli, because although the Senegal coucal occurred in the drier west of Kenya I'd never seen it in all my time in Amboseli.

Then there was the slide of the chanting goshawk. The pale one was often seen at Amboseli, but Carpenter described his as the dark chanting goshawk. I had to agree that although the slide was not as clear as that of the coucal, the bird did indeed look like the dark one. And the rosy-breasted longclaw – the slide illustrated beautifully the soft pink breast of this unmistakable bird. I remembered it from the dry plains of Tsavo National Park east of Amboseli, and again in the dry west of the country, but I'd only heard of the yellow-throated longclaw being recorded from Amboseli.

Carpenter also made reference to having seen a scaly francolin at Amboseli, though he didn't have a slide. This too would have been a new record, but I was prepared to doubt even Carpenter's identification here. Francolins are notoriously difficult to tell apart unless you get an excellent view, or better still have a dead bird to look at.

My other nagging feeling came with some of the slides that showed the broader habitat as well as the birds in it. Most were close-ups of birds that could have been anywhere, but a few showed vegetation and contours and they didn't strike me as a hundred per cent Amboseli. Quite flat grassy plains, and not as many swamp pictures as I would have expected. However, there are similarities between a number of Kenyan game parks, so maybe that wasn't a fair comment.

But by the end of the talk I was having distinct doubts about Carpenter's ethics. He was presenting all these slides as his own, but it seemed more than likely that he'd borrowed extra ones from colleagues, perhaps of the American and Asian ones too. And if he was so untruthful about these, how much reliance could be placed on his alibi for Charles Pendleton?

And where had Marion got to?

Marion was sitting with Dirk Pienaar's student, deep in conversation.

'I hope you were paying attention to the talk. What did you think of Carpenter's slides. Did you notice anything odd about them?'

'Not really. I thought they were pretty good on the whole.'

'I mean the African ones, considering they were all supposed to have been taken in Amboseli.'

'Oh, you mean the dark chanting goshawk? It certainly did look like the dark.'

'I quite agree. And what about the rosy-breasted longclaw?'

'What about it?'

'Not allowed in Amboseli either.'

'I didn't twig on that one. I'm sure we saw one in Tsavo. That's not far away.'

'And what about the scaly francolin?'

'Yes, I spotted that, but he didn't have a slide of it. I just assumed he hadn't had too good a look at it. You know what *francolins* are like.'

'He didn't make too many mistakes in Suikerbosrand. I think there's something fishy about it all. I reckon he's borrowed slides from other sources and tried to pass them off as his own, which is a bit much when he makes a point of claiming to be such a good photographer. And if we can't trust him on that, can we trust him over Pendleton's alibi? Perhaps the two of them in reality had a nice ivory poaching trip. Carpenter getting a look at the action for once?'

'Hm.' Marion was looking thoughtful. 'I must say I wouldn't mind seeing the rest of his 'Amboseli' slides. He told us the other night he had them with him. Just to see how many other fiddled ones there might be. Do you think we could get him to show them to us?'

'You might be able to get him to show them to you. He seems to have taken a fancy to you. If he doesn't want to it might be a sign of guilt. If we're lucky...'

'Okay, I'll see what my fluttering eyelashes can do.'

They went into the lunch room, and Marion walked

over to the buffet table where Carpenter was heaping up his plate.

'Those were *marvellous* slides,' she said. 'I haven't seen such a consistently good selection for a very long time. Didn't you say you took quite a few more at Amboseli besides those?'

'Sure, I've got a stack. I just didn't feel I could put them in because they weren't relevant enough to my theme. I was already off it too much as it was.'

She turned her sweetest and most appealing gaze on to Carpenter. I thought she was overdoing it to hell, but he seemed to lap it up.

'Oh, do you think – would there be *any* chance that we might be able to see them?'

Carpenter looked a bit disconcerted, and my antennae bristled.

'Sure...' he said doubtfully. 'If you're staying for a few days more, that is. I can't do it now because Dirk Pienaar's about to take me to the Kruger National Park for three days, but the day after I get back I'm due to show them all to the Witwatersrand Bird Club. They're holding a special meeting in the Biology Department at the University. Seven thirty on the fifteenth. I reckon they should allow you in as my guests, and you'd be very welcome.'

'Thank you so much, we'd love to do that...'

Carpenter's initial reluctance seemed to have a valid reason, but I was still a bit suspicious. More direct evasion tactics would have been better, though. Carpenter's departure also meant *yet* more delay. Crime detection was obviously as slow and painful as scientific research.

After lunch we joined the stream of delegates booking out of the Hotel Egoli. We decided we might as well move closer to the university since we no longer had a car, and we took a taxi to the one large hotel in the suburb of Braamfontein.

This proved to have another large conference running at it, and all they could offer us was two single rooms at opposite ends of a long corridor. The rooms were clean and cheap and we were fed up with moving around, so we accepted.

It was a decision that had dire consequences for Charles Pendleton.

_ 25 _

In the morning we were faced with three more days to spend in Johannesburg. We decided first to have a look at the university, which from Marion's hotel room window could be seen a little way up the road. We wandered out into the street and dawdled along, looking into shop windows and at the multitude of Africans around. Anyone would have thought that Braamfontein was a black suburb, with African delivery men carting boxes into shops, house-maids out with their shopping bags standing talking on the pavements, black flower-sellers and newspaper vendors at the street corners, even a black parking meter attendant.

And beggars, like a blind African woman sitting motionless on an upturned milk-crate by the door of the local supermarket, as expressionless as she was sightless, a small tin resting on her lap. I watched her for some minutes while Marion went back to the hotel to fetch a letter to post, and was interested to see several black people put money into her tin as well as a few of the passing whites. I found that moving, for a reason I don't think I could explain.

Then I noticed the boy selling newspapers near where I was standing. He pulled out a paper packet containing two slices of dry bread. He put these together carefully like a sandwich and ate them. No jam, no butter, nothing.

I thought with a guilty conscience of the huge Middle Eastern meal we'd eaten two nights before, that had probably cost what this boy would earn in a month or more, and had provided me with a great surplus of unnecessary nourishment. Again I felt irritated at how this country could keep getting me to betray my principles. But would it have been any better or worse, I thought, if I'd eaten it in England? I'd have done it there with no qualms. Perhaps this place is making me some sort of hypocrite.

I walked over and dropped several large coins into the blind woman's tin, but I didn't feel any better.

Marion rejoined me, and we walked through the portals that proclaimed the entrance to the University of the Witwatersrand. The buildings were a hotchpotch of styles from neo-classical to geometrical, but the campus had a pleasant, open feel to it, with large trees scattered at intervals. The conference that had just finished had been organised then because it was university holidays, but in the southern hemisphere this wasn't the long vacation and students were already filtering back.

Some were wandering round with books. Others were putting up posters for the Jewish Society, the Campus Union for Christ, the Wits University Historical Society. I noticed a number of garish placards advertising a lunchtime meeting in two days' time to protest at government-inspired evictions of Indian and Coloured people from two Johannes-burg suburbs. I was surprised to see such meetings allowed in public, which was not the impression I'd had from the British press about political freedom in South Africa.

Spotting the biological departments, we walked inside and up to the library to look at the display of journals. However, there was nothing that hadn't already been in our libraries at home before we left. Then Marion said:

'Dirk Pienaar's student works here. I might just drop in and have a look at his equipment for handling birds of prey.'

'I think I'll go and wait outside in the sun. I'm a tit man myself....'

Marion either missed this comment or chose to ignore it.

I sat in a sunny nook on a wall and watched university life flow by. A gang of Africans, stripped to the waist and glistening with sweat, were straining at a hoist to lift a huge air-conditioning unit to a first-floor hole in the wall. Two white supervisors sat on a wall and offered abusive advice at intervals. One looked swarthily Portuguese, his skin darker than the lightest of the Africans. I was reminded of Jan and how he addressed his Africans, but somehow this was different. With these two the element of goodwill was missing, and I doubted that Jan would have sat by entirely while others did the work.

Some time later Marion came out with Dirk Pienaar's student.

'Mike's offered to take us to a good place for a sandwich

lunch,' she announced and swept on towards the gates, leaving me to hurry to my feet and follow. Marion could always get up a good speed when food was involved.

We passed a small restaurant with two distorting mirrors outside, one labelled 'Before' which made you look short and fat and the other 'After' when you became tall and thin.

Mike said: 'That's Mangles, if you're looking for a good cheap eatery while you're here. They do nice fricadelles, and a superb fresh banana drink.'

But we passed Mangles and went to the next corner where there was a shop called Bread and Butter. This contained a mouth-watering array of sandwiches and rolls filled with unusually imaginative mixtures of ingredients.

Marion chose a huge roll called a Vrystaater, containing a piquant curried mince. Mike picked one with avocado and green pepper. I peered down the list, and my eyes lit up when I discovered bacon and banana. My twin addictions in one roll – heaven!

We perched on a wall outside and munched. I said:

'You know, I'd have trouble remembering I'm in Africa here. Apart from the climate and level of sophistication, I might just as well be in Brixton. There are about the same number of black faces in both.'

'Yes, you really have to go to the homelands before it begins to look like traditional Africa,' replied Mike. 'Even Soweto's just a poor, scruffy, overcrowded European type of city. But there are elements of something different even here. Have you ever been to Diagonal Street?'

We shook our heads, so he said:

'Why don't we go there next? I have to drop an advert in at the Star newspaper office in town. It's nearly on the way.'

We walked down through Braamfontein, over the cluster of railway lines converging on Johannesburg station, and past the African bus station with its teeming throng of black women, walking with perfect poise so as not to unbalance the shopping bags on their heads. I saw one woman carrying an ironing board on her head, which required more gymnastic feats to maintain, and I couldn't help chuckling at another who just had a can of soft drink perched on her bonnet.

We came to the glass and concrete composition of the new Johannesburg Stock Exchange. Then, in the shadow of this symbol of white economic strength and domination, we plunged into another world as we entered a thin street running diagonally to the others.

But though un-European, it was scarcely African either. Rows of tiny shops with Indians at the open fronts; pavement sellers with little heaps of fruit set out on mats or trolleys; cheap and thin cotton clothing; random heaps of pots and pans. It reminded me of films I'd seen of streets in Asia.

At one end stood a row of African taxis, labelled 'Second Class Taxi' on the doors. Large battered American vehicles whose opulent style no doubt gave prestige to driver and passenger alike. It probably also entitled the owner to charge more, and certainly allowed more passengers to be crammed into the capacious seats on the journey to and from Soweto.

Ours were the only white faces among the black and

brown, and we received some curious glances. For my part I gazed with interest at some of the shop displays. There were assortments of European and Asian pseudo-pharmaceuticals, with ambivalent slogans suggesting they would help flagging sexual energy. There were skin-lightening creams, ginseng tonics, vitamin pills, almost anything.

Seeing me looking at the skin-lightening creams, Mike said:

'Sad, isn't it? There's nothing wrong with a black skin, but there are always some that want to make it lighter. Those ones have a mercury ingredient that's banned by law. For medical reasons, not political ones,' he added with a faint grin.

It was all rather sad, except perhaps to the vendor who could probably make his fortune from such sales. Especially of some, which I wouldn't have minded betting were placebos and had cost him almost nothing.

More interesting further down was the shop of an African herbalist, selling what Mike said were *muti* or traditional African medicines. Through the tall glass windows were rough wooden shelves, stacked with bottles of seeds, dry leaves, pieces of bark, powders, snake's vertebrae, animal teeth, and a host of unidentifiable remains. Above them hung dried and gnarled roots of all sorts, old tubers, skins and assorted animal remains and much more that the eye couldn't take in at one perusal. Inside the shop were many more shelves with further specimen bottles reaching up the wall, and the ceiling was festooned with more twisted roots, snake skins, animal hides, hyenas' tails and other bits that defied description.

The shop was very dark, with a musty but not unpleasant smell, but the old man inside gave us such a baleful stare we felt uncomfortable and left.

As we came back out into central Johannesburg Mike turned and said: 'You probably don't know the local prices well enough to compare, but the Africans could buy those same clothes, pots and pans, and fruit and vegetables for less money in the OK supermarket in Braamfontein. It's not only the whites who exploit the Africans.'

* * *

Such diversions helped to pass the time, but by the third day of waiting we were getting a bit edgy.

'I think I'll go in to the University at lunchtime to see Mike,' said Marion. 'He told me he'll be doing a post mortem this afternoon on one of his birds that died recently.'

'I may as well come too,' I said. 'Not much else to do.'

As we approached the University I could hear the sound of a public address system, and seeing a throng of people at the central square I realised it was the lunchtime of the protest meeting.

'Actually I think I'll just go along and listen,' I said. 'It'd be interesting to see how far people really can go with free speech in this country.'

I left Marion at the biology building and wandered over

to the plaza in front of the Great Hall. A man on the steps beneath massive pseudo-classical columns was gesticulating energetically and shouting into a microphone. He was flanked by several other people, evidently co-organisers of the protest, and a large crowd had gathered to listen, almost filling the broad square. Quite a few of them were black. The crowd was sympathetic to the protest for there were cheers and shouts of approval, and frequent clapping as points were made.

At the back I could see a man with a telephoto-lensed camera recording the scene. With his burly frame and pencil-line black moustache he didn't look like the typical news photographer, and he seemed mainly concerned to take individual shots of the people who were most vocal.

The main speaker finished with some extra loud exhortations, and the crowd stamped and whistled and began a rhythmic handclap. A group of Africans along one edge raised their hands in black power salutes, and started to sing something in African. I turned and asked the student next to me what it was.

'Oh, that's "Nkosi Sikelel'i Afrika" – God Bless Africa. It's the national anthem of the Transkei homeland, man, and it's the hymn of the African National Congress. You probably know they're banned – the authorities are going to love this.'

As the singing swelled, the photographer put down his camera and spoke into a small radio that he pulled out of his pocket. Within less than a minute powerful, over-revving engines could be heard, and two Hippo riot-control vehicles followed by four armoured personnel carriers roared up the road beside the Engineering department, sirens screaming.

The leading vehicle smashed straight through a chain barrier across the end of the road, uprooting two concrete pillars and flailing broken ends of chain through the air. It screeched to a halt beside the square. Helmeted police in combat dress, carrying sticks and transparent shields, poured out of the wagons and raced into the crowd. Others with Alsatians were running in from the opposite side of the square, and mesh-sided trucks for the removal of prisoners were drawing up behind the personnel carriers. A show of force had evidently been intended, and it was stunningly effective.

The Africans had suddenly evaporated. No doubt in Soweto they had plenty of practice at it. Not so the whites who were jumbling in aimless confusion, more concerned to dodge the batons than to escape. But one black youth tried to run out past me and was grabbed by a policeman.

I shouted angrily: 'Let him go! He hasn't done anything wrong!'

Stupid, of course, but it was an instinctive reaction. I found myself immediately pinioned from behind.

I was dragged tripping and stumbling to one of the wire-meshed wagons, and pushed unceremoniously into the press of bodies. Others bodies quickly followed. A minute later the door was slammed and padlocked, and the truck drove off.

MARION

_ 26 _

Inside the laboratory I could hear an increasing sound of an amplifier and what sounded like a loud harangue going on outside our building.

'What on earth's that? It sounds rather like a revival meeting.'

Mike looked up from the abdominal cavity of the eagle that he'd been dissecting.

'I think it's politics rather than religion. There've been some posters up for a protest meeting about evictions of Coloureds and Indians. We have meetings like that every now and then. They usually go for about half an hour and then fizzle out. And nothing more happens, of course.'

The loudspeaker continued, audible above the snipping of Mike's scissors. But then there was a sudden sound of sirens. The loudspeaker stopped, and a general hubbub of voices, yelling and screaming took over.

'What on earth's going on out there?'

'Sounds like the police have come to arrest the speakers at that protest meeting. They usually do it sooner or later. It's a quick way of breaking up a meeting. They interview them at John Vorster Square, knock them around a bit, cool them off for a few hours. Then they let them go, without charging them usually. Most haven't done anything illegal anyway. But it does sound like they've gone to town on this one.'

'I hope Nico'll be all right...'

'He should be, unless he was up on the steps speaking. He'll probably be here in a minute to tell us all about it.'

But he wasn't.

After a while I began to feel a bit of niggling concern. The idiot might just have been idling on the wall again, but I thought I'd better check.

As I went to a corridor window that looked towards the Great Hall, two students were passing. One said to the other:

'Man, did you see the cops? They're really pushing it this time, busting up a meeting inside Varsity like that!'

'Why, what happened?' I asked.

An uncomfortable surge of alarm had spread through my system.

'Oh, there was a protest meeting outside the Great Hall, and the cops busted it up and arrested hundreds of people who were listening. Jeez, they really went to town, I can tell you! It looked like '76 in Soweto all over again.'

'Christ...'

I walked numbly out of the building, trying desperately to think what I should do if Nicholas wasn't there. But my thoughts were too scrambled.

The police had departed from the forecourt of the Hall, which now contained a few disconsolate people standing around or talking, oddments of rubbish and belongings dropped by fleeing or arrested persons, and scattered spots of drying blood.

Nicholas was nowhere to be seen.

I felt a sick feeling in the pit of my stomach. I needed to closet myself to think more clearly, so I withdrew to the Biology Women's toilet. I sat on the seat for quite a while, attempting to recover calmness and rationality.

Nico might just have wandered off somewhere to waste time, though *surely* he wouldn't have done that if he'd realised that I must have heard the uproar. If not, he must either have been injured or arrested. Unless he'd wandered away before the trouble and didn't know about it himself. If only I knew which....

Should I phone the police? No, safer to ring round the hospitals....except they'd be in touch with the police, if the injuries were from the meeting...

Eventually I decided it would be dangerous to call anyone who might report to the police, because if Nico had indeed been arrested the police might be intending to take action against him. If I contacted them they might seize me as an accomplice or something. The vitally important thing was that at least one of us should get to Byron Carpenter's slide show tomorrow evening. I couldn't afford to contact the police, and if I was really unlucky they might already be looking for me.

If I do get arrested I won't be able to help Nico anyway, so he'll have to look after himself. Fortunately he's fairly self-reliant. My main worry is that he'll tell the South African police what he thinks of them. He doesn't always know when to keep quiet about his principles.

I didn't feel like going back to Mike. Not that I didn't trust him, but I wanted someone older and more experienced to lean on for advice. Perhaps I should go to the British High Commission? No, that's in Pretoria. There's a Consulate in Johannesburg...but maybe they'll be all correct and hand me to the police if I'm wanted.

It will have to be someone unofficial. Samaritans? Salvation Army? Not really in their line. Perhaps a churchman. But can you trust even them in this country...?

And then I suddenly remembered Carina. She's the elder sister of Jan du Toit. She came to Aberdeen once when Jan was going out with Moira, and I had instinctively liked her. She and I still exchanged Christmas cards, so she should remember me.

I was sure Carina's address was a Johannesburg suburb, but which one? It begins with an 'E', if I remember right...

My address book was back in the hotel and I didn't want to go there in case the police were watching. I remembered passing a public telephone on the Biology ground floor. Perhaps it would have a phone book with it.

I left the sanctuary of the toilet, and went cautiously downstairs. There was a phone book chained to the wall, and I hastily flipped through the list of suburbs with their abbreviations at the front. Elandsfontein, Elsburg, Electron; no, it was more like an English placename than that. Edenvale,

Ellis Park, Emmarentia...none of the 'E's rang a bell.

I looked further and my eye lit on Houghton. That was it, surely! Now, what was Carina's married name? She was divorced from her husband, who'd disapproved of her liberal sentiments and even more of some of her actions, but she hadn't reverted to her maiden du Toit. It was another Afrikaner name...

After a moment I remembered it was Viljoen.

To my dismay there were several pages of Viljoens in the directory, and none with a first initial 'C' lived in Houghton. Of the whole collection only four had Houghton addresses, and none of those had any 'C' among their initials. Of course the phone might still be in her husband's name, but I couldn't remember what that was. What was the address? It was a block of flats, but all of these sounded like flats. If only I hadn't raced through my Christmas cards so quickly...

There was nothing else for it – I'd have to ring all four. What coins did the phones need? Five cent pieces. I could only find one in my handbag. I dialled the first Houghton Viljoen, and when the number answered I said quickly:

'Hullo, is that Carina Viljoen who used to be Carina du Toit?'

I was answered with a voluble burst of Afrikaans, after which the phone was put down.

I scrabbled through my coins for more of the tiny five cent pieces, but there were none. Shuffling feet came down the corridor towards me, and I stopped an elderly African janitor.

'Could you possibly give me some five cent pieces for the telephone? I can give you some change,' I added pleadingly.

He looked at me suspiciously, then sought deeply in his baggy uniform trousers and pulled out a leather purse. He opened it slowly and poked around, and came out with one five cent piece. In relief I pressed several larger coins on him. He inspected these carefully and dourly before pocketing them and shuffling on.

I dialled the second Viljoen. There was no answer.

I dialled the third number. It was answered by a plain 'Ja?'

'Hullo, is that Carina Viljoen who used to be Carina du Toit?'

'Yes...' The voice sounded wary.

'Oh! It's Marion MacTaggart here. You remember, we still send each other Christmas cards. I met you when you visited Jan in the UK, do you remember?'

I realised that I was gabbling somewhat, but I was desperate that Carina wouldn't ring off. I had no more coins.

'Marion! How nice to hear from you. Are you here in Jo'burg?'

Her intonation had the slight musical lilt that I'd noticed in other South Africans speaking English.

'Yes, I am. I wondered if I could possibly see you to ask your advice about something?'

'Yes, of course...er, are you all right?' She must have registered by then that I was sounding rather odd.

'Well, sort of, but I am in a slight spot of bother.'

'Where are you at the moment?' The voice was authoritative now.

'I'm at a public phone on the ground floor of the Biology department of Wits University.'

'Okay, wait at the front door of the Biology department and I'll pick you up in ten minutes at the most. Houghton's quite nearby. All right?'

'Thank you so much,' I said rather limply.

I put the phone down and wondered for a moment if Carina or the police would turn up. Then I decided the thought was quite unworthy. It was terrible how paranoid you could get in this sort of situation. I was probably making a great fuss over nothing anyway.

Carina arrived quickly, and with the minimum of greeting whisked me into her car and back to her flat in Houghton. She was a tall, slim and elegant woman, about late thirties in age. In contrast to her brother who had a strong accent, she spoke flawless, precise English with a clear and melodious voice. She was the sort of person who made heads of either sex turn, and an air of reserve heightened her allure rather than diminishing it.

The flat matched its owner in elegant simplicity, and the chairs were very comfortable. Carina put me in one with a small glass of brandy, and we sat in silence for a few moments. Then she said:

'You sound as though you've had a good welcome to South Africa. What happened?'

There was a slight sardonic edge to her enquiry.

'Well, it was all going quite well until today.'

I told her about Nicholas, the demonstration, and how I particularly needed to go to the Bird Club's meeting, though without explaining the significance of Professor Carpenter's slides.

But Carina was no fool.

'You don't have to tell me the details, but I take it there's a special reason for going to *this* slide show, rather than all the others that must be available to you in your profession...?'

She looked at me with cool grey eyes.

'Yes, there is. I may as well tell you.'

So I launched into the story of the ivory and the Masai spear murder. At the end Carina said:

'Thank you. I like people who're prepared to do something for a cause, and that's a cause I approve of. I'll start making some enquiries for you.'

'That's very kind of you, but I don't want to get you into trouble with the police or anything.'

Carina gave me the same faint, sardonic smile as before.

'My own cause is the freeing of our black people,' she replied. 'I do a lot of work with the Black Sash movement. I doubt if you could get me into more trouble than I'm in already. Now the first thing is to find out what your hotel says. What was Nicholas's room number?'

'Two three six.'

Carina looked up the Braamfontein hotel number and dialled it.

'Good evening. May I speak to Dr Twistleton, please?

He's in room two three six.'

There was a long pause, then: 'No message, thanks. I'll try again later.'

She turned to me.

'They say there's no reply from the room. So at least he didn't just miss you and go back to the hotel. I suppose the next place is the police station.'

She didn't have to look up that number. When it answered she spoke in Afrikaans, asking various things but apparently getting no reply. She put the phone down again.

'They say they've never heard of Meneer Twistleton. No record anywhere on their books. Don't worry!' she added, seeing my look of dismay. 'That's probably good news. Would Nicholas have been carrying any identification on him?'

'Yes, we always keep our passports on us overseas.'

'Well, the first thing the police do is produce a list of injured persons after a demonstration, in case there are repercussions over any of them. The man was obviously looking down a list of those names, and I'm sure Nicholas would have been on it if he'd been hurt. When I asked if he might be in police custody the man just said: 'We have no record of Meneer Twistleton'.'

'Heaven knows what that implies,' I said.

'I think what it probably means is that they arrested so many people today they haven't finished processing them all yet. With whites it's usually only on pretty serious charges that they deny having the person when they've actually got them.'

'What do you think they'll do to him?'

'Not very much, especially when they find out he's an overseas visitor. They don't want unnecessary bad publicity. They'll probably just give him a talking-to and release him again in the morning. Though if he argues with them or if they're feeling very bilious they might deport him. I presume you must have had return tickets on you to be allowed into the country?'

'Yes, his ticket would be in his hotel room, I think.'

'Well, I suppose it wouldn't be complete disaster if that happened. You at least would still be able to go to the slide show. Now I think it would be best if we waited until morning before doing anything more. Would you like to spend the night here? I'm sure you don't want to go back to the hotel after all this.'

'It would be nicer. But what if Nico turns up back there?'

'I'll leave a message with the hotel for him to wait there until morning. They won't know who sent it.'

She rang the hotel again, then said: 'Good! Now come and help me get some supper.'

We went into the kitchen, and Carina dug out a frozen packet of mince.

'To help you see one of the better sides of South Africa I'll teach you how to make bobotie. It's an example of two of our cultures interacting positively. Cape Malay spices meet the shepherd's pie, you might say. Now, we're going to thaw this mince, then curry and spice it, then add raisins and nuts, then put it in a casserole. You'll find a large glass one in that cupboard just behind you. Then we pour a savoury custard over the top and bake it...'

She chattered on for a while about the influence of Malay servants from the Dutch East Indies on Cape cookery. She was obviously used to coping with people who were upset.

As I lay in bed that night I wondered why I should be feeling quite so shaken up. I'd always considered myself to be fully self-sufficient, but I was actually missing the quiet, slow presence of Nico more than I'd expected.

I must have dozed off before I decided whether that was a good thing or bad.

* * *

In the morning Carina rang the hotel again, and was told that Dr Twistleton had checked out. He had left no for-warding address.

'It sounds as though the more pessimistic of my guesses has come true. I think they're chucking him out. We'd better go round to the hotel and see what happened.'

We drove over to Braamfontein, and parked in a side street near the hotel while Carina went in to investigate. She came back after about five minutes and said:

'The management was very tight-lipped. I don't think they like things like that going on at their hotel. They wouldn't tell me anything, but I went upstairs and found the Zulu chambermaid. She told me the police came round about six o'clock this morning. The manager let them into

Nicholas's room. She said the white boss, meaning Nicholas, wasn't with them. They threw everything from the room into the suitcase and took it away.

'It's a stroke of luck that you were in separate rooms. As it is, nobody seems to have connected the two of you. I couldn't see any police around. Why don't you go up and collect your belongings and check out – move into my flat until you leave? I can take you to the Bird Club tonight. I quite enjoy natural history slides!'

'That's very kind of you. I certainly wouldn't mind. I don't really fancy staying on alone in the hotel in the circumstances. Would you come in with me in case anything happens while I get my stuff?'

'I don't think that would be very wise since I've just been asking about Nicholas. You'll be all right – there was nobody untoward around.'

I went into the hotel with some trepidation, but nobody seemed to give me a second glance. I packed my suitcase quickly. At the desk they asked why I was checking out early, and I mumbled something about an earlier flight back to London. I gave my father's name as a forwarding address.

My heart was still pounding as I got into the car and we drove back to the flat.

'One last phone call, I think,' said Carina. She dialled the police number again. After a further conversation in Afrikaans she said: 'I am informed that Meneer Twistleton has been declared *persona non grata* in the Republic of South Africa. He's at Jan Smuts Airport awaiting a suitable plane to leave the country.

'I think we'd better leave it at that now. They already wanted to know why I was asking after him. I said I'd met him at the recent biological conference and wanted to discuss the habits of impala with him. You should have heard what the policeman said about that. Don't worry, he'll be okay. There are plenty of people here who've run foul of the South African Police and would give anything to be in his present position at Jan Smuts.'

I realised with some horror that that would be true.

In the afternoon Carina had to go to a meeting. I opted to stay in the flat, feeling it would be safest.

'This is a bad area for burglary and mugging,' said Carina. 'Don't open the door to anyone, and don't answer the phone unless it gives a funny series of rings first. That'll be me trying to get you!'

Left to my own devices in the flat, I wandered over to the bookshelves that ran down much of one wall. The books had clearly been bought for interest or love, not for display. Their owner had catholic tastes, but the dominant theme was a love of Africa. Picture books of South African and Rhodesian scenery, faces of Africans, faces of Boer pioneers. Literature in Afrikaans and English, poetry in Zulu; a dictionary of South African English, an Afrikaans-English dictionary, and a Dutch-English one. Even a Setswana-English dictionary tucked away at one end.

Other slim volumes of poetry were in English, but by black African authors. I picked a book of short stories by

Herman Charles Bosman, written in English but about rural Afrikaners at the turn of the century. I was much moved at how the author could tell a story so simply, and in it combine gentle mockery with obvious affection for the human frailty of the people he was writing about. It was a plane of existence that somehow had been lost in the hundreds of years of civilisation of Europe.

After a while I got up to stretch my legs, and I walked around the rooms of the flat. It wasn't that I wanted to invade Carina's privacy, but I was curious to understand this coolly enigmatic woman better. But the flat gave away little. As with the books, nothing had been arranged for display. The effect was one of quiet sophistication, but the true personality of the owner was as hidden as it was with the owner herself.

The phone rang, starting and stopping twice, then continuing to ring. It sounded like the definition of a funny series of rings, so I picked it up.

'Hullo, Marion? It's Carina here.'

'Hi, Carina.'

'I'm terribly sorry but it looks as though I'll be home later than I expected tonight.'

My heart sank.

'I promise you I'll be back by ten to seven, though. To save time do you think you could have a meal ready for us by then? You'll find eggs in the fridge for omelettes, bacon too and a few other bits and pieces. I'm sorry to do this to you, but it is rather important. I promise I won't stand you up. I'll do it for the elephants.'

'That's okay. See you at ten to seven then. Goodbye.'

'Thank you so much. Bye!'

I was filled with misgivings that things were going to go wrong over this evening. Still, I reasoned that if Carina didn't get back in time I could always ring for a taxi from the flat. I had plenty of money left – just no five cent pieces.

I started making the filling for the omelettes at six o'clock. Much too early, but I had to do something to take my mind off the fact that Carina might be late. At quarter to seven I began the omelettes, and as the last was almost ready the door opened and Carina came in. She looked tired and drawn.

'Hullo there. What a delicious smell! It's nice to come home to something cooked ready for you.'

She poured herself a small shot of brandy and gulped most of it down, then quickly washed her hands and came to the table.

Over the quick meal she said: 'It wasn't only you and Nicholas who got in a mess after yesterday's protest meeting. Two Black Sash committee members were arrested and haven't been released yet, and we've been trying to sort out a lot of personal problems of Africans who had relatives of some sort disappear. The police seem to have been especially thorough and vindictive this time. I think they're trying to put an end to that sort of meeting by intimidating the potential audiences.'

We gulped down our meals, had a further quick wash,

and drove off to Wits University. To my immense relief, we arrived at the campus five minutes before the meeting was due to start. We parked by the Psychology building and walked across to Biology.

The building was in complete darkness, and all its doors were locked.

_ 27 _

I gaped in amazement. My first thought was that Professor Carpenter had had a guilty conscience about letting us see the Amboseli slides and had cancelled the meeting, but reason told me that was ridiculous.

'I can't understand it,' I said, totally dismayed. 'I can't possibly have made a mistake about when it was.'

'What exactly did he say about it?' asked Carina.

'He said it would be on the fifteenth, which is today, at seven thirty in the Biology Department of the University.'

Carina looked at me blankly, then suddenly shouted: 'Oh my God, it'll be at RAU! Come on!'

We raced back to the car, and as we roared down to the university entrance, crashing over the speed humps in the road, Carina said:

'There are two universities in Jo'burg. The other one is the Rand Afrikaans University. They tend to use it for this sort of meeting because it's got better lecture halls and pro-jection facilities than Wits. It's not all that far, but I'll have to take care not to get stopped for speeding. They're pretty hot in this area.'

She drove only slightly above the speed limit, but when the traffic lights at a junction in Auckland Park went yellow she put her foot down and gunned through a light just red. Very shortly afterwards a large motorcycle cut across her front with a touch of its siren, and a gauntleted hand waved her in to the kerb.

The policeman came slowly and ponderously to the driver's window of the car.

'Good evening, madam. Are you aware that at the junction back there you committed an offence by driving your motor vehicle through a traffic signal showing a red light?' His speech was as ponderous as his walk, and heavily accented.

Carina answered him in Afrikaans, but he didn't bat an eyelid. The conversation continued in Afrikaans, culminating with the patrolman pulling out his pad. He went slowly to the front of the car, and it took him a while to enter the make and registration number. Then he had to fill in the date, time, nature of offence, name and address of the driver, names of all the roads involved, direction of the offending vehicle. There seemed to be an awful lot of apparently relevant information.

The policeman must have been instructed to write in careful capital letters, or perhaps was unable to do anything else. Then he insisted on doing a full check of the car's lights, horn and tyres, which luckily were all in order. Finally he tore one sheet from his pad and handed it to Carina, with a lot more Afrikaans that sounded like what to do with it, or maybe it was just a lecture on not driving through red lights. Then he returned to his bike, wheeled it round and roared off down the road, most certainly in excess of the speed limit.

'*Ag sies, man*!' said Carina, as she wound the window up again. 'Of all the unlucky times for that bastard to be lurking. I'm sorry, I seem to be doing my best to make you miss this meeting.'

'What did he give you?' I asked, my heart still pounding from shock, as Carina continued more carefully down the road.

'On the spot fine. Probably twenty rand. At least it wasn't speeding. The penalties are a lot heavier for that. Sometimes they let you off if you talk to them in Afrikaans, but not this one. A real heavy.'

We drove past a sign reading Rand Afrikaanse Universiteit, and up to the visitors' car park, which fortunately still had empty spaces. In front of us was a modern and quite striking building of rough natural finish, stone and glass, but there was little time to admire its architectural qualities. We sprinted up the broad pathway and in through a huge glass door.

'Waar is die Voëlsvereniging?' panted Carina to the elderly caretaker inside.

He pointed down the long corridor. 'Roltrap C, tweede vlak.'

We raced along the echoing tunnel, its high walls

finished with a deliberately rough surface and covered with enormous pipes feature-painted in bold colours. Under other circumstances it might have been an exciting effect, but at present I just found it eerie.

We went up the escalator marked C to the second floor and followed a sign reading Bird Club, through double doors into a beautiful and plush lecture hall. We were nearly half an hour late for the lecture, but to my amazed relief I saw that Professor Carpenter was still sitting at the side of the rostrum. An elderly man was wittering on from the floor about construction arrangements for a new hide at one of the East Rand ponds.

I'd actually made it!

As we took our seats the chairman, almost as though he'd been waiting for us to arrive, moved to interrupt the elderly speaker and say that the matter should be adjourned until the next meeting. He then introduced Professor Carpenter, who mounted the dais as the lights went down...

_ 28 _

Carpenter began by apologising for the fact that his lecture would be little more than a slide show of 'pretties'. He was sure he had less practical experience of African birds than anyone else in the lecture theatre, but some people had been kind enough to say they liked his pictures and thought a wider audience might enjoy seeing them.

He said a few introductory words about Amboseli, and projected his first slide which was a fine view of general scenery. The country was more rolling grassland than most of Amboseli, but there were certainly parts like that and I didn't know all the reserve. Pendleton had obviously taken him to some out of the way corners. In the distance in the view was a low range of hills – not as spectacular as the massif of Oldoinyo Orok, which at about 8,300 feet is a spectacular feature of Amboseli, but maybe he hadn't been able to get a shot of that.

After this came the bird slides. Some I had seen during the conference address, but a lot were new. And as before they were superb pictures, but some were anomalous. Peters' finfoot, for example. A difficult bird to photograph well and Carpenter had caught it beautifully, but it shouldn't have been at Amboseli. Likewise the eastern grey plantain-eater, the black and white-casqued hornbill, the lemon-rumped tinker-bird, and the arrow-marked babbler.

I was beginning to share Nico's view that Carpenter must have cheated and included other people's shots as well as his own, but was puzzled because the slides looked so much as if they were part of one single series. They were very similar in composition, lighting and tones of colour. Usually when pictures are from several cameras, there are more obvious differences. Perhaps Carpenter's cheating had been different. Maybe he'd made more than one visit to East Africa after all. Been to more reserves than just Amboseli, but was trying to pass himself off as a novice.

And then it was that the true explanation and its devastating significance hit me. It was the seed of this last thought combined with Carpenter's following slide that did it.

'My next picture is one of which I'm particularly proud,' said Carpenter. 'It's a bird you all know well from South Africa, but I wonder if you've ever seen it quite as close as this!'

And the screen lit up with a dramatic explosion of vibrant scarlet and black. The bird was finch-sized and had the broad, squat beak of a finch. It had a jet-black face with a shiny eye in the middle, and then scarlet over the rest of the head, including a ring under the chin. The rest of the bird, appropriately called a Red Bishop, was brilliant red and jet black, like black robes against the red of a cardinal or bishop. The bird stared at us with haughty disdain from its perch on a reed, like an opulently clad mediaeval prelate on his throne. That prelate had never resided at Amboseli, but he *did* live in Masai Mara...

And a simultaneous but silent explosion blew Pendleton's alibi to pieces, as I realised that Carpenter had never been to Amboseli. At least not on that trip with Charles Pendleton.

He had only been to one Kenyan game park, and that one was Masai Mara.

It *had* to have been... I mentally ticked off all the anomalous features, and it all began to fit together. In numb amazement I missed the next three slides, but when I focused again on the fourth it confirmed my idea beyond doubt.

The picture showed a large cluster of yellow-billed oxpeckers, which did not occur in Amboseli, perched at various angles on the sides and head of an antelope that from its colour pattern, and its almost vertical, lyrate horns, could be nothing but a topi.

And the only park in Kenya that had topi was Masai Mara.

I couldn't resist seizing Carina by the arm.

'I've just realised what happened!' I whispered, more loudly than I meant to. 'Carpenter was deliberately misled about which park he was taken to. He actually went to Masai Mara, I'm sure, which means Pendleton's alibi is a load of rubbish. It has to be right!'

'They're lovely slides,' murmured Carina, who'd been asleep and hadn't heard a word.

The slides clicked their way on, and with them my mind. After the initial elation of scotching Pendleton's alibi it occurred to me that Carpenter had not necessarily exonerated himself yet. The deception could still be his, in passing off slides that he knew were taken in Masai Mara as being from Amboseli, and this might have been deliberate deception to help Charles Pendleton. An American might not have realised how much the bird fauna could vary within a short distance on the ground in East Africa. It was more likely that he'd been duped, but I couldn't risk alerting him if he were guilty until some more significant people had also seen the slides. People like Malcolm Gibson and Ezekiel, the Nairobi police inspector, if possible.

I wondered if there was any possibility that I might be able to entice Carpenter to Kenya.

The slide show finished with rapturous applause from the audience, and a generous speech of thanks from the chairman. As the audience drifted away I left Carina, who was sound asleep in her seat again, and I went up to the stage.

Carpenter spotted me immediately.

'Hi, Marion, I'm glad you could make it! I looked for you at the start.' He peered around. 'Where's Nicholas?'

'He had to...er...go back to Kenya in a hurry. I'm really sorry he couldn't have seen those slides – they were absolutely superb!'

I could at least say that in all truth.

'I know a lot of people in East Africa who would love to see them. Is there the slightest chance you might be able to come up there while you're in this part of the world? I could probably raise the money to cover the extra cost to you, and you could have a look at some other Kenyan game parks.'

Like Amboseli, where you were supposed to have been...

I watched him as I made the offer, but he didn't look in any way concerned. He thought for a moment.

'Well, I guess it might be possible....in fact that's not a bad idea. I was booked to fly to London by your British Airways next Sunday, and they just advised me today they screwed up the booking. I might be stuck here for several days longer because of pressure of traffic. They can damn well get me as far as Nairobi on some flight or other, and we'll work it out from there. At their own expense, too – you needn't worry about that!'

I hadn't even had to flutter my eyelashes at him.

'Oh, that would be marvellous if you could! I'm going back now as soon as I can, but I'll wait till you know when you're coming, and I'll tell you how to contact us up there.'

'Great! I'll get on to the airline first thing in the morning and then ring you. You still at the Hotel Egoli?'

'Er, no, I'm staying with a friend at the moment. Just hang on a minute while I get the number.'

I went back and woke Carina to get her number, then wrote it down for Carpenter.

'Okay, I'll be calling you in the morning. Good night!'

'Good night, and thank you again.'

I escorted a still dreamy Carina from the lecture hall and back to the car. On the way out she said: 'I did enjoy that very much', from which I deduced she hadn't heard anything I'd said about the significance of the slides. I decided it could wait until morning.

Over breakfast I said to Carina:

'I don't think it registered when I told you last night, but I owe you a very great debt of gratitude for getting me to that meeting.'

And I explained how things had turned out even better than I'd expected, and we now had grounds for disproving Pendleton's alibi.

'That's marvellous,' said Carina. 'I'm afraid I was only taking things in at a rather low level last night. What are you going to do now?'

'I've tried to persuade Professor Carpenter to make East Africa his next stop, so I can get some of the people involved in the case to see his slides. It would stand up much better in a court of law if the police could give direct testimony instead of having to rely on a statement from me. He's ringing me here as soon as he's seen the airline about changing his flight. If he gets it, I'll have to go like a bat out of hell to get an earlier flight so I can get to Nairobi before him and start setting things up.'

'If it happens this morning I can take you out to Jan Smuts,' said Carina. 'I'm not doing anything till late this afternoon.'

She sounded a little wistful.

'A pity you can't come too,' said Marion. 'You look as though you could do with a break. You'd really love East Africa, I'm sure you would.'

Carina gave a little laugh, but without humour.

'I'm sure I would too, but I don't think the Kenyans would love my South African passport.'

I felt myself blushing. I'd entirely forgotten about such considerations. An awful image passed briefly across my mind, of being trapped in the problems and tensions of South Africa as a conscientious objector without any possible means of escape.

At that moment the phone rang. Carina answered, and waved it at me.

'It's your professor.'

Carpenter had been busy, and had already managed to get on a plane leaving tomorrow night. I gave him Peter Marston's telephone number and told him he could contact Nicholas there. I had no idea if Nicholas actually was there, but I could send Peter a warning telegram if I couldn't get a flight ahead of Carpenter.

I wished Carpenter a pleasant journey, and rang off.

'I'd better get straight down to the airline office to see if I can convert this open ticket for a flight tonight.'

'I suggest we go to a travel agent. I know a good one. She'll be prepared to ring around much more widely than an airline to get you on a flight.'

This proved a good suggestion because there was a lot

of trouble finding an empty seat at such short notice. I wondered if all the seats had been commandeered by the South African Police for people being expelled from the country. In the end I had to buy a new single ticket to get the only flight that still had a vacancy for today. The travel agent assured me I could claim back for the other unused ticket once I was back in Nairobi.

Carina insisted on taking me to the airport after I'd packed my case. On the way I said to her:

'Maybe if you can't come to Kenya you can still come and see us in England some time. Though it's not the same, of course.'

'Thank you, it would be nice, but I think my place is really here with my people. Until we get everything sorted out – if we ever do...'

'You've been so helpful over my cause and I haven't done a thing for yours. I haven't even asked you about it to try to understand it.'

Carina smiled a wan smile.

'I don't suppose it would have done you much good. You have to live a lifetime in South Africa to understand the country, and even then most still don't.'

She paused for a moment.

'If you really want to try, I suggest you read the books of André Brink, especially one called 'A Dry White Season'. He's an Afrikaner who's come closer than anyone I can think of to understanding South Africa and capturing its feel. He's a very brave man, for he doesn't like what he sees, and many here don't like what he writes.'

She appeared then to go into a private reverie. I rode with her in silence.

At the airport we had a glass of wine in the bar lounge, and I tipped out my remaining South African money.

'Please take this as a donation to the Black Sash movement to defray its expenses in getting the anti-ivory movement to the meeting last night.'

I was glad to note that the amount was more than the twenty rand of the fine.

'I couldn't possibly accept it – please keep it!'

She was quite vehement, but I gave her a hard stare back.

'It's not from me. It's from the elephants.'

She looked at me for a moment, then smiled faintly.

'Okay, for the elephants….'

We walked to the security gate that led to the check-in area.

'Goodbye,' said Carina, holding out her hand. 'Please don't forget those of us in South Africa who are still fighting for our cause.'

I suddenly couldn't say anything. I took Carina's hand and pressed it. I could walk out of the problems so easily while others stayed to face them, against very unfavourable odds.

I went through the barrier, then turned and looked back at the tall, isolated figure, whose face had already closed up. We waved, and parted.

_ 29 _

The atmosphere at Nairobi Airport was once more warm and balmy, a pleasant change after the nip of late winter on the highveld. I was through airport formalities by ten o'clock, and immediately rang Peter Marston's number.

'Hullo, Marston speaking.'

'Hullo, Peter, it's Marion here. Do you have Nicholas with you?'

'Yes. He's just having a shower before going to bed.'

'Thank God for that!'

'He didn't smell that bad.'

'Idiot!' The relief in my voice must have been obvious. 'I meant the fact that he's with you. He'd vanished off the face of the earth as far as I knew. Listen, I'm at Nairobi Airport at the moment. Tell Nico when he comes out of the shower that he's not going to bed, he's coming out to the airport to pick me up. I've got some exciting news, and we've got some quick planning to do for tomorrow.'

An hour later a well-scrubbed Nicholas appeared at the airport. I was surprised at the warmth of his embrace.

'You great idiot,' I said. 'Fancy getting thrown out of a paradise like South Africa!'

'Some paradise. I'll tell you about it in a minute.'

'Yes, I'd be interested to hear your version,' I said, rather drily. 'I heard part of the South African Police's version of it. But I'd better tell you my news first because we're going to have to act on it quickly.'

Back at the Land Rover I found Peter as well.

'Oh, hi, you shouldn't have bothered to come as well at this hour!'

'No problem, I thought it might be useful for the planning that you mentioned. Thought I'd leave you to see if you still recognised each other in the airport, though.' He was grinning mischievously.

As we drove off down the airport road I said:

'So have you discovered the flaw in Pendleton's alibi yet?'

Knowing full well they wouldn't have.

'No,' replied Nicholas. 'We've found out something else of interest about him, but not that. You had an illuminating time in South Africa, then?'

'Yes, literally. It was the illumination of Carpenter's slides that did it. I realised that Carpenter never went to Amboseli.'

There was stunned silence in the Land Rover, palpable even above the noise of the engine. I enjoyed my moment to the full.

Finally Nicholas said:

'So where did he get all those slides then?'

'In Masai Mara, of course. Where the Senegal coucal may

be found in the bush country of the west of the reserve. Not to mention the dark chanting goshawk, the rosy-breasted longclaw, and the scaly francolin even. There were several other anomalies that cropped up during the latest showing, all of which are known from the Mara.

'And at the start he showed one general scenic shot. I couldn't place it as anywhere in Amboseli, and when I finally twigged about the birds I realised it had been a typical view of rolling hills in the Mara. The flash of inspiration came when he put on a red bishop. You really must see that one, by the way – it's a fantastic shot. And the clincher came when he showed a bunch of yellow-billed oxpeckers on a topi. Now refute that!'

'Well, it sounds plausible.' Nicholas paused. 'But how on earth did he get there? Pendleton's plane went to Amboseli.'

'Ah! I've been thinking about that too. Remember the Amboseli flight log? The plane was booked down as arriving late. But Carpenter told us they left Nairobi early if anything. They went from Nairobi to Masai Mara first.'

'And how did Pendleton's plane then get to Amboseli?'

'Do you remember Carpenter's description of their arrival? They landed at a spot where there was no proper airstrip, in other words Pendleton didn't want their arrival to be seen, and they left the plane in the care of an African. You can bet your life it was Peter Motokwe. Jerry Szymanowski told us he's got a pilot's licence. And on the return trip they just switched the opposite way.'

'Mm...plausible, I grant you. That would also explain

why nobody saw Carpenter during his visit. He had to be kept isolated or the deception would have been discovered.'

'Exactly. The only one who could be fooled was Carpenter himself, who'd never been to East Africa before. He'd believe whatever he was told. He'd see birds that he'd know to be East African, but he wouldn't be likely to know the detailed distribution park by park unless he had check-lists of the reserves' faunas. I haven't asked him about that yet, but I'll bet the answer will be that Pendleton didn't give him any. Or maybe mocked one up showing Masai Mara birds listed as Amboseli.'

'Jesus!'

There was silence again as Nicholas and Peter digested my ideas.

'That explanation accounts for another thing that had been bugging me unconsciously ever since Carpenter described his flight,' I continued. 'You know we've flown down to Amboseli a number of times. You're usually throwing up or something, but I like to look out of the windows to spot landmarks and animals and things, and I'm always annoyed by the way one has to squint into the sun to do it.

'But Carpenter said the flight was marvellous because the sun was right behind him. I didn't stop to work it out at the time. I just thought he'd had a luckier time of day or something. But if you think about it, they left early in the morning and a plane flying from Nairobi to Amboseli is travelling south-eastwards. You *must* have the sun fairly well into your eyes on the left side, and it wouldn't be behind you on either side. But from Nairobi to Masai Mara you're flying west. Sun rising directly behind you, right?'

'Right. It certainly does seem to fit together.'

'The one thing I haven't been able to check yet is whether Carpenter was left alone on the day of the murder. I can't remember what he told us about the times Pendleton left him to get supplies.'

'I can't remember offhand, but I made some notes when Carpenter was talking to us that day. They're back in Peter's house – I'll check as soon as we get back. I have a feeling he did leave about then, but I wasn't really paying attention because I was still thinking in terms of Pendleton having to fly across to Masai Mara.'

'Well, that's my news. Did you say you have something too?'

'Yes, but it's not as exciting. I thought I'd try to do something constructive once I was back here, so I went into Nairobi this morning to check on the registration of a certain company, namely coffee growers called Ruiru Highland Plantations.'

'And….?'

'There are three directors registered. There's a husband and wife called Dennis and Joyce Smythe. I've since found out that they live on the estate and run it. The interesting thing is that maiden names are given, and Joyce was née Pendleton. And the third director is one Charles Albert Pendleton. Could that just possibly be someone we all know and love?'

'Can't be two of the bastards...'

'That's what I thought. Then I looked at other companies owned by Ruiru Highland Plantations. They actually own Huntsman Safaris. They also own the Swaziland Import-Export Company in Siteki. More than that, they own several nightclubs in Nairobi and Mombasa, including – you guessed it – Ebony and Ivory in Mombasa.

'I made an appointment this afternoon to see Ezekiel – he came to the New Stanley again. I told him what we'd found out in Botswana and Swaziland, plus this new information. He said he'd send someone up there to keep an eye on goods moving in and out of the estate. I think he was going to try and get him on the staff as a labourer, to get some hard evidence.'

'That would certainly tie up that side of it nicely.'

'Sure would. I hope we don't have to wait too long before the next shipment of ivory arrives there. Not that I want more elephants slaughtered specially, of course. But what was the urgent planning you said we had to do right away?'

'Ah, yes. Well, it did occur to me that although it looks as if Carpenter was hoodwinked about which Kenyan park he visited, there's still a chance he was party to the deception and is in the poaching along with the others. I thought it would be best if we could get him up here to show the slides once more, and make sure the audience includes people like Ezekiel, Malcolm Gibson and anyone else that matters. There couldn't be much dispute about the evidence in a court of law then. I've persuaded Carpenter to come here

– he arrives in Nairobi tomorrow evening. What we have to do now is arrange some accommodation for him, and a plausible meeting at which he can show the slides.'

There was a pause, then Peter who had so far been silent said:

'The accommodation won't be a problem, and I can probably help you over the meeting. Leave it with me tonight, and we'll work something out first thing in the morning.'

* * *

It was very late when we got back to the house, and we decided to go straight to bed. Tucked into the sheets, I nestled against Nicholas and said:

'How are you, Nico? What did they do to you?'

'Not much, really. I suppose it was my fault. I was only watching the protest when the police moved in, but I shouted at a policeman who was arresting a black youth and told him the lad hadn't done anything wrong. So they grabbed me too and threw me into a van with a mass of other people.'

'Yuk!'

'Yes, it was a bit 'yuk'. It got hot and stuffy very quickly, and we all got stiff because we couldn't move properly, and I think the person who was pressed against me wet himself. It wasn't me, anyway.'

'Did they put you into cells?'

'Sort of. We were all herded into rooms that were locked, and then nothing happened for ages except we were given some horribly milky tea and some bread. Eventually they came and started taking people one at a time from our cell.'

'Did they interrogate you?'

'Well, it was just questioning, really. I quickly told them I was a visitor – maybe that influenced things. I said I'd done nothing except call out when I saw an innocent black youth being arrested, and the police captain, who was a real nasty smoothie, said what gave me the right to judge that he was innocent.

'His manner made me angry, and I asked what gave him the right to judge that the lad was guilty of anything for just listening to a public speech. I suppose it wasn't very tactful. Anyway, he didn't like it. He gave me a lecture on how outsiders couldn't understand the problems of South Africa, how we were all hypocrites, how we just came to stir up trouble, how the blacks were much better off and happier under a benevolent white government than anywhere else in Africa.

'That last bit made me sick, and I said "I suppose they love hanging out of police station windows by their ankles".

'That did it. He went icily calm and told me that people with my negative attitudes were not welcome in the Republic of South Africa and I would be deported as soon as possible. I was put back in a different cell, and in the morning they brought my bag to me. I had to give them money to pay the hotel, and they had my airline ticket amended for a flight that afternoon. They took me to the airport where they kept me under supervision in a back room, and finally escorted me on to the plane to make sure I went.

'It was so lucky that we had separate rooms at the hotel. I realised during the first long wait that if I didn't say anything about you they wouldn't connect us, and I was just praying you wouldn't come storming down to the Police Head-quarters or something and get arrested as well. That's why I didn't try to send you any message once I got back here. I figured it would be safest for you to leave you entirely alone.'

'Yes, you were right there. I was very lucky – I got in touch with Carina Viljoen, who's Jan du Toit's sister, and she looked after me the whole time. I think without her I probably wouldn't have coped. She's a brave person. She's taking on the system, without the safety net of deportation like us. I'm not sure I'd have the courage.'

'Yes, I must say I found the whole thing unnerving even though they didn't actually do anything to me. There was this pervasive feeling of menace all the time. But I think the worst were the screams. There weren't many of them and they were fairly distant, but I really learned the meaning of one's blood running cold. I used to say that a hyena's call sounded chillingly human, but I was wrong. There's no animal call like a real human scream of pain or terror.'

We lay silent with our thoughts, and I realised what lay behind the haunted look that had sometimes been in Carina's eyes.

She had seen and heard it all too.

_ 30 _

I woke in the morning to the sound of Peter Marston singing in the shower, on the other side of our evidently thin bedroom wall. It was not an award-winning performance, and not a good way to start a day.

Nicholas had disappeared. When I got up I found him rummaging through his book of notes on our meeting with Carpenter. First he pulled out a newspaper cutting.

'The original report said Fergus was murdered on a Thursday evening. Now let's see, yes, here we are. Pendleton left Carpenter late in the afternoon on Monday, Wednesday and Thursday – about half an hour each time, but possibly more on the Thursday – up to an hour. That would have been enough, surely!'

'I reckon it would. I think Pendleton's alibi is well and truly finished now.'

We joined the family for breakfast. After the tribulations of recent days Monika's competent motherliness was very welcome. It was like waking from a bad dream to find you are in your own bed after all.

When we'd eaten, Peter suggested we go round to the research station offices. He ushered us into the Director's room, which was about the same size as Nicholas's office in England and quite a bit smaller than mine.

'I'm Acting Director again,' he said. 'It'll be handy for organising this meeting because there are two outside phones in here. I thought the best might be if we hold your meeting here at the station. We've got quite a nice little lecture hall that we use for farmer education classes, and we just acquired a cracking new projector the other day. It'll be a chance to christen it.

'I can also guarantee you a moderate-sized captive audience from here, and I'm sure we'll be able to rustle up others. The main thing is to make sure that the date suits both Ezekiel and Malcolm Gibson. I definitely think both of them ought to be present. Could one of you try to get Malcolm on that phone? There's the number.'

Nicholas made the call, and after some delay obtained Malcolm on a bad line and explained the situation to him. Peter meanwhile spoke to Ezekiel on the other phone. It transpired that the first mutually convenient date was not for another five days, but after a hasty discussion we agreed to book the meeting for then.

'That's a bit of a blow,' I said, as they rang off. 'What if Carpenter can't stay that long?'

'We'll just have to try and persuade him,' said Nicholas. 'Why don't we offer him a few days in the real Amboseli to help pass the time?'

'I wouldn't do that,' said Peter. 'You wouldn't want to draw attention to the deception till after the meeting. If you take him to Amboseli he'll realise it wasn't where he went before, and if you take him to the Mara he'll probably recognise it. But the general idea's not a bad one. Why don't you tempt him with a few days up Mount Kenya? That's an offer a biologist really can't refuse. I know the warden up there, and I'll guarantee to get you hutted accommodation if Carpenter will go.'

'Now that really is a suggestion,' said Nicholas. 'I've only been there once myself.'

He looked at me. 'You can put it to him. You seem to have him eating out of your hand these days!'

* * *

Carpenter's plane was more or less punctual, and he seemed pleased that we were there to meet him.

He was less pleased when I told him en route to the research station that he would love to stay in Kenya for another six days, but he began to soften as I described the biological delights of Mount Kenya. I emphasised what a unique habitat it was – a chance of a lifetime to take him there – how lucky we'd been to get the opportunity to take him up there…. Nicholas told me afterwards that I was right over the top, but I must have still been Carpenter's favourite girl because he accepted.

'Aw, what the heck! I said I'd be back at the Museum next

week, but it's vacation time on campus and I'm sure they can do without me a bit longer. I guess the airlines'll play ball. They still owe me a favour or two. I'll come.'

Carpenter spent the night in the guest room of the research station, and breakfasted with the Marstons. I was feeling guilty about the amount of hospitality the Marstons were providing, and I urged Peter to let us contribute for Carpenter's stay.

Peter looked right down his nose at me and said:

'It's costing us so much to keep the two of you here I doubt we'll notice the difference'.

We fitted Carpenter out with field station overalls since he'd brought no field clothing. We packed food and sleeping bags and set out in the Land Rover for Mount Kenya.

We detoured into Thika for Carpenter to buy film in anticipation of new birds to photograph in the park. Along the way we saw a prominently signposted entrance to Ruiru Highland Estates. I glanced at Carpenter as we passed, but his face showed no sign of recognition or interest.

We continued north through Muranga and Kiganjo, and just before Naro Moru we turned right off the main road towards Mount Kenya. Unusually for so late after dawn, the mountain was still more or less cloud-free and we could see its flattish contour soaring impressively from the plain below, surmounted several small blips like nipples on a shallow breast. The view was quite impressive – perhaps a good omen for the trip.

'Gee, that's a fine-looking mountain,' said Carpenter.

'It's just over seventeen thousand feet – the second highest mountain in Africa. The highest is Mount Kilimanjaro, which is another two thousand feet up. But you would have seen that from Amboseli, of course?'

Knowing full well that he wouldn't because he was in Masai Mara from which it isn't visible.

'Well, I sure don't recall it, but I'm not sure that I would have known it.'

'You'd have known it all right if you'd seen it – it's a spectacular broad mountain with a permanent snow-cap on the top. Though to be fair the snow is often hidden by cloud.'

We drove on through farmland and plains to where the country became wooded, and rose through increasingly thick stands of juniper and podocarpus. The podocarpuses were fruiting, and we saw – and photographed – a fine group of red-headed parrots feeding on the fruits. We eventually arrived at the park gates, each with a metal silhouette of a rhinoceros hinting at exciting prospects within. An ancient skull of an African buffalo was fixed to a post by the entrance, bleached white bone and huge, curling black horns, staring vacantly at all who entered.

And the next three days passed most pleasantly. We managed to show Carpenter a great variety of vegetation, which gradually changed as we rose in altitude. At first there were huge, gnarled trees and dense forest thickets that must have been immensely old, and higher up many of the trees were covered with abundant strands of lichen, trailing downwards like old men's long beards or a grossly exaggerated hoar-frost. Then we reached a bamboo zone, and above that hypericum scrub. The hypericum still had some flowers, which were attracting a lot of scarlet-tufted malachite sunbirds – deep green of malachite combined with vivid red flashes on either wing, and very thin tails as long as the birds themselves. Even Carpenter got quite enthusiastic about those. We also saw large molehills thrown up by the giant Mount Kenya Mole rats. I'd never seen the animals themselves and this time was no exception, but the hills were still impressive.

Finally we reached a zone of more open moorland. The driveable track stopped at about eleven thousand feet – after that it was travel on foot only. I think Carpenter would have been game to go on, but sadly we didn't have the time though we did manage a bit of a trek up through the 'vertical bog' on the steep, open hillside, with pretty orange gladioli and orchids growing wild upon it, up to the level of the weird giant senecios and lobelias.

We oscillated between the park headquarters beside the gate and a small wooden rest hut at ten thousand feet. It was hard to see many birds in the thick forest, but up in the higher bamboo we saw plenty. Carpenter watched the birds and took huge numbers of photographs, and he was watched in turn by elegant black and white colobus monkeys. They peered at this curious sight before swinging and leaping away through the tall bamboo trees like a troupe of acrobats, their haunting calls – half howling and half grunting like an over-loud frog – resounding around the forest.

We were interested to watch the great photographer in action. He would open his neat aluminium attaché case in which each item of equipment was set in its own slot in a foam rubber bed, take out what he needed, and then he would immediately be in another world. He was oblivious to all around him except for the target bird, and he would wait with infinite patience for the perfect pose.

This often-prolonged immobility enabled us to see more animals than the average visitor. Shy bushbuck or duiker would materialise from the trees, without a sound and with only the movement giving them away. Once in the bamboo forest we had our first sight of that most elusive of all antelopes, the bongo. I thought at first it was a particularly large and brightly coloured bushbuck, until I realised it was far too big and I remembered that the bongo occurred there. It came half out and stared at us across a thinner patch of the bamboo, its white stripes clear against its handsome chestnut body, its horns and white facial marks camouflaging its head against the vegetation. Then with a flash it was gone again, alas not to return to have its portrait captured.

We also saw one great bird rarity – high up in the forest we found an Abyssinian Long-Eared Owl, which is very rarely seen. I was interested to find that even Carpenter didn't know that one, and I have to admit that I only realised what it was because I'd done my homework on the bird list before we went. Carpenter did, however, know Mackinder's Eagle Owl which we also saw – a large bird with a fierce expression and fiery orange eyes, described in my book as the finest of East African owls and they weren't wrong.

Back in the resthouse in the evening, we thought it might be interesting to see what Carpenter's views were on wildlife poaching in general. We'd agreed that I would kick it off while Nicholas watched his reactions.

'We get awfully worried here in Africa about poaching of animals and birds, but I guess you've been exposed to the same in the Americas?'

'I surely have. It's a problem everywhere – South, Central, North America – you name it. But I've had the most exposure to poaching in Central America. I'm an advisor to Congress on the subject, and I've helped various governments over birds like curassows, guans and some parrots. They're all quite spectacular birds, and aviaries in lots of places are after them. I could name you at least a dozen each of mammals and birds that are regularly poached, and half a dozen or so reptiles. Some of these are now endangered as a result.'

'So what can we do to try to reduce or stop this trade?'

'Sadly, not enough. You've gotta have good legislation for a start, to define what's protected, and you've gotta have good penalties in place. That's handy for the rather rare times when you catch someone. You also need good surveillance of wildlife at risk, which the governments say is too expensive and there are too many to watch them all, and the poachers simply bribe the watchers anyway. Then you've got to try and stop the trade, which is maybe the most effective way, but there are plenty of ways of circumventing that too.'

'You're dead right about the importance of trade. We've been focusing on that in the efforts to stop poaching of elephant ivory, but the smugglers are still finding ways to get the ivory out, and plenty of markets aren't too worried about the quality of the certification.'

'I think that's one of the more tragic examples of poaching. When I was in Amboseli I saw my first ever elephants in the wild, and it quite took my breath away. They're so majestic – there's something about their scale and grandeur that other animals just don't have. Though I guess I'd have to say that a jaguar in full hunting mode in South America is also pretty damn impressive too, and they get poached just for fur coats.'

The conversation drifted on a little, and then turned to the habits of curassows that were obviously Carpenter's favourite birds. We both said afterwards that it was good that he gave us that run-down because we'd never even heard of curassows before.

We also agreed that he seemed to be quite genuine in wanting to stop any forms of poaching and to protect wildlife – especially his new favourites, the elephants. And he didn't seem to be evasive or embarrassed or anything about the whole discussion. We decided that he deserved any benefit of doubt in relation to his alibi for Pendleton, and he appeared to have been deceived on exactly where he was taken. It would be interesting, however, to see what his reaction would be when he found out about the deception...

_ 31 _

A t the end of the three days Carpenter expressed himself well pleased with the visit, and our quiet observation of him suggested that he did know his birds really well, and he was a decent and honest man with an apparently genuine commitment to nature conservation. So far so good, and we all returned to the Marstons' in good humour. Next day Carpenter photographed yet more birds around the research station, until late in the afternoon visitors began to arrive for the slide show that evening. Monika and Peter had organised a buffet supper for the benefit of those travelling from afar, and it gathered momentum with lively informality as guests drifted in.

Malcolm Gibson arrived with several other park biologists, including Jerry Szymanowski from Amboseli, who lost no time in reminding Carpenter how he'd been one of his more brilliant students. He waved a bottle of bourbon several times, but Carpenter said he'd better wait until after the screening.

Peter Marston circulated as the perfect host, chatting to

every guest individually. I discovered later that he'd actually been warning each one in turn not to get up during the screening and point out the Amboseli/Masai Mara anomaly.

Ezekiel arrived with two other Africans as people started to drift over to the lecture hall, and the audience was swelled to a respectable size by the last-minute arrival of a minibus from Nairobi, containing ornithological members of the East African Wildlife Society and a few staff from the university zoology department. Peter, knowing they were on the way, had lain in wait so that he could extend his warning to them too. He knew that some of the keen bird-watchers would have been on to the geographical discrepancies in a flash.

Carpenter delivered his show to a mounting chorus of oohs and aahs and gasps from the floor, and the acclaim at the end showed the audience to have received it just as well as in South Africa. They dutifully avoided any questions about locations, and the few questions were technical ones about equipment and techniques.

As soon as it was over Peter said:

'I wonder if we could just have a word together in the next room?'

Carpenter looked a bit surprised but agreed. He looked rather more surprised when he saw Nicholas, Malcolm and me coming too, plus Ezekiel and his two companions.

Noticing his increasingly suspicious looks I felt I'd better say something quickly.

'We owe you a fairly handsome apology, especially as you

yourself have been treating us so generously. But please may I ask you one question first? When you were in Amboseli with Mr Pendleton, did he give you a checklist of the birds of the park?'

Carpenter didn't have to think about that. 'No, he didn't, and I thought it was a bit unprofessional of him. In other respects he ran a good show, but not with that. I would have brought one myself if only I'd known, but it never occurred to me that that wouldn't be part of a specialised bird-watching trip.'

'Okay, we had a reason for getting you to come here other than just to give people the chance to see your slides, although the reception tonight should have shown you how much they appreciated that too.'

I was picking my words as carefully as possible.

'We wanted you to show them while you were under a misapprehension that we could have corrected, but didn't for reasons we'll explain in a moment. It has relatively little significance for you, but a great deal for someone else.'

And I proceeded to explain the geographical misrepresentation, to mounting incredulity and then bemused fascination on Carpenter's face.

There was a short silence after I'd finished, then Carpenter said:

'Jesus! I sure am glad to be able to nail that sonofabitch for you. I've said before I'll do anything to stop game poaching, but, hell, I've got a personal grudge now as well. He's made me look a fool in front of three meetings now. It sure bugs me to present wrong information, even if it wasn't entirely my fault. I guess I should have checked out some distribution lists when I got back to the States last time. And my secretary's going to murder me!'

Puzzled faces greeted this last comment.

'Three hundred and twenty-eight slides that have to be re-labelled. She'll kill me....'

I remembered the immaculately labelled slides we'd seen in Johannesburg, and realised that the secretary did indeed have grounds for justifiable homicide. Perhaps we should send her after Pendleton.

'Thank the Lord I discovered this before National Geographic printed them. Jesus, I'd have been the laughing stock of the world.'

He turned to face all of us.

'May I ask what you guys propose to do about this now?'

'I guess that's up to Ezekiel,' said Nicholas.

He introduced Ezekiel who in turn introduced his companions as members of the anti-poaching unit of the Kenyan Police. The senior of these, called David Kambatini, spoke.

'I think that tomorrow morning we should pay a call on Mr Pendleton. When your information came in the other day we checked on him, and he was still in his camp at Mara Reserve. Malcolm, you would probably like to come with us?'

Malcolm nodded. 'I surely would!'

'Hell, I'd be more than happy to come along too,' said

Carpenter. 'If you'd allow me, that is.'

Kambatini considered for a moment.

'Yes, that might not be a bad idea,' he said slowly. 'It would be a nice confrontation for Mr Pendleton.'

He looked at Nicholas and me. 'I think that Dr MacTaggart and Dr Twistleton have also earned the right to come, if you would like to? It would not be a bad thing to have many people.'

* * *

Next morning our party set out, across the same route that we'd taken not many weeks before, but our feelings were very different this time. I wondered what a showdown of this sort would be like. Dramatic and violent, as in any good work of fiction, or flat and anticlimactic as seemed more likely in real life?

In practice there was no showdown of either sort. When we pulled into the Huntsman Safari permanent camp area we found no vehicles, and a quick check of the tents revealed no people either. After a short consultation we withdrew behind some trees and settled down to wait.

It was the absolute definition of an anti-climax.

_ 32 _

Charles Pendleton was particularly irritable that morning. In fact he'd been irritable for days now. There'd been the sudden late safari cancellation by the Japanese tour, which was why he had no customers in the camp at the moment. Then there'd been the regular reports by Peter Motokwe of the infuriating pair of biologists snooping round their operations, and Motokwe's bungled attempt to stop them.

He'd probably have to call a halt to the ivory shipments for a while until things cooled down, but with the safari business slack he couldn't afford the loss of the ivory income.

The only bright spot on the immediate horizon was the giant tusker that had recently come across the border from Serengeti – at least he'd never seen that one in the Mara before. That would be his one treat and consolation. He certainly wasn't leaving one like that to the Somali trackers.

While he was thinking these dark thoughts Peter Motokwe came into the tent, just back from his latest delivery to Ruiru.

'Is okay, boss, I deliver it all safely. But there was a man with the labourers there who was police spy, I think. He ask me too many questions about the boxes. But don't you worry, boss, I fix it okay this time. They never find his body now, for sure!'

'You WHAT??' roared Pendleton.

Motokwe looked taken aback. 'I fix him,' he said, making a throttling motion with his hands. 'I put the body in the furnace. He is all gone now.'

'You bloody stupid kaffir, you've really wrecked it now!'

Pendleton had gone purple in the face.

'If that man was a police spy it means they know something about Ruiru. When he disappears they're really going to go to town. Christ alone knows why I pay you money when all you do is sabotage my operations!'

Peter Motokwe seethed with cold fury inside. This arrogant white man dared to talk to him, Peter Motokwe, like that. Calling him a stupid kaffir when the Kikuyu cook in the next tent could probably overhear. It had been bad enough when he'd reported the misfortune with the car explosion. This man should not have been so angry at his bad luck then. But now, when he'd done exactly what had been required of him before! He would not forget, or forgive. Arrogant white pig. May the hamerkop shit on his tent....

* * *

For Charles Pendleton it was the final straw. Everything would have to be moved out of Ruiru quickly now, and the whole operation put into mothballs for some time – perhaps even relocated. *How maddening, how absolutely maddening. But he wasn't going to let it spoil the giant tusker for him. The beast might not still be in the Mara if he didn't get it now. There should still be plenty of time before anyone came down this way to investigate.*

He called Peter Motokwe back in.

'Get yourself and the Land Rover ready. We're going after one more bit of ivory before I close it all down and sack you for a while.'

Motokwe felt his gorge rising again, but decided to bide his time. Pendleton came out with his elephant gun and cartridges and laid them in the Land Rover beside the smaller rifle and ammunition that he carried on safaris as a safety precaution. They drove off towards the remote corner of the reserve where he had last seen the elephant. They came across several herds meandering and gently browsing, until he suddenly motioned Motokwe to stop. He put up his binoculars, and there he saw it. The dream of every elephant hunter!

He reached out of the window and held a little wind-vane above the vehicle roof, then motioned Motokwe to drive quietly to the downwind side of the herd. As the vehicle stopped one or two elephants glanced idly at it, but it was some way away and they continued feeding. One in particular stood out from the rest – a large animal with a huge and striking pair of tusks, not only very long but almost completely straight. A pair like that, shipped whole, would be worth an absolute fortune on the Far East markets. You could just about name your price.

When the animals had settled again they opened their

doors and climbed quietly out, Pendleton carrying the gun and Motokwe a box of ammunition. The animals made no move, so they began carefully to stalk them. Charles Pendleton's blood thrilled with the excitement. Just like the good old days. This was the life.

They were certainly both experts, and they got very close to the large bull before Pendleton decided enough was enough and he had better take it. He motioned to Motokwe, who handed him the box of ammunition.

Pendleton opened it, then whispered quietly but venomously: 'You absolutely bloody incompetent fool, these are the small ones for the rifle. Christ, you blacks don't have a brain in your bloody heads! Get back to the vehicle and fetch the others, and hurry up about it or the beasts will have moved on.'

He was fuming with anger and impatience, but he was not fuming nearly as much as Peter Motokwe. This was the final insult. He'd show this white slime what he thought of him.

He went back to the vehicle and got in, but instead of reaching into the back for the other box of cartridges he slammed the door, started up the engine, tooted loudly and waved at Pendleton, and drove off.

Pendleton was so astounded that for the first time in his hunting career he completely forgot his situation and all the rules. He whipped round and stood up, yelling:

'You ignorant black bastard, what the HELL do you think you're doing?!'

The elephant, which had already become alert as the car door slammed, reacted sharply to this threatening animal rearing up in front of it. Its ears stood out, its trunk curled up and its feet pawed the ground. It trumpeted, and it charged.

Pendleton instantly realised his mistake and began to run. He could feel the pounding footsteps vibrating the ground ever closer. He twisted and hurled the useless gun at the elephant, but it didn't even notice.

He tried to swerve but the elephant struck him violently in the middle of his back, and he sprawled flat upon the ground. The elephant stood beside him panting and shuffling for a minute, then decided there was no longer any threat. It moved slowly back to join the herd, snorted a few times, and resumed its feeding.

Pendleton lay on the ground numb with shock, feeling a dull pain in his back. He would have to keep quiet until the elephants were safely away from him, then walk back to the track and hope he met a car rather than a lion or leopard or something. And God knows what he was going to tell them when they picked him up. He'd have to bury that stupid gun, too – it could be traced to him. What a waste, an awful waste. He'd been very fond of that particular weapon.

He kept his eye on the slowly receding herd, and when he had recovered his wits a little and judged it to be safe, he made to get to his feet. At which point he discovered that he could only move his head and his arms. There was no feeling in the lower part of his body. He was paralysed from the waist downwards.

He tried several times with increasing panic, but there was no doubt about it. He couldn't move.

He lay back in a violent sweat of fright. Now he really was in trouble. He would be at the mercy of any wild animal that might find him there. Perhaps he could drag himself with his arms as far as the rifle, and use it like a club to protect himself if anything came along. But what on earth would happen to him?

It was a million to one chance that anyone would drive to that exact spot and find him lying there, at least before he had died of starvation and thirst. With a sudden spark of hope he thought that maybe Peter Motokwe would relent and return, but his heart told him that the chance of that was also a million to one. Against.

Motokwe couldn't know, of course, that he was lying there alive but paralysed, but the bugger probably wouldn't care anyway. Treacherous black bastard. He'd never trust any of them again...but, oh God, if only he could have the chance to try.

He lay with his mind casting in all directions for some possible way out of this awful plight, when out of the corner of his eye he saw something that filled him with even greater horror than anything his mind had yet conceived.

A brownish-black band about nine inches wide was approaching him, trickling and tumbling over the ground like a tongue of muddy water, flowing slowly but relentlessly forwards. Even before his eyes could focus on the individual insects he knew he was looking at the front end of an army of siafu – a column of countless millions of driver ants, known and feared by all who had ever seen them. They had plundered and devastated the land around their last bivouac, and were now on the move to look for new shelter and fresh food.

With great heaves of his elbows he dragged himself through the dust until he was well clear of their path, but as the leading ants crossed the groove that his body had left in the soil they paused and began to meander around, piling up and tumbling over one another. Some explorers ran along the furrow, perhaps attracted by the animal smell he had left in it, perhaps just following an easy path. When they discovered the inert flesh the message was transmitted back with the uncanny speed that ants can manifest, and rapidly the whole column wheeled and flowed towards its next repast.

Pendleton had collapsed with the exertion of his movements, and it was only as he felt the tickling of the insects on his face and the needle-sharp mandibles slicing into his flesh that he came to again. He brushed wildly at his face, but more ants fell off his arms. Then he looked at his bare legs beneath his khaki shorts and saw them black and heaving. He gave a great scream and attempted to roll and crush them, to drag himself further on, to brush them away, anything.

His panic-stricken writhing killed tens of thousands of the ants, but the scent of their crushed comrades aroused the others to a greater frenzy of activity, and they redoubled the ferocity of their onslaught. Pendleton passed out again from combined shock and over-exertion, and nevermore recovered consciousness.

Siafu *generally take smaller prey than humans – small mammals, birds and many sorts of insects. However, they are quite willing to take larger animals if these are immobile, and Charles Pendleton was a good find. It was quite a few days later when the advance party of the column moved forward again, while the last of the ants ran up and down the bones looking for final morsels that had been missed. Eventually they too moved on, and Pendleton's immaculately cleaned skeleton was left to bleach in the sun.*

_ 33 _

By early afternoon our party had begun to suspect that our vigil might not be rewarded. Inspector Kambatini went to the park office to telephone instructions to Nairobi. He ordered road blocks on the major roads out of Masai Mara, and surveillance of other major roads in Kenya, especially to the coast and westwards to Burundi. He also had his office alert authorities in Tanzania to watch for Pendleton and Motokwe.

He returned to brief us on these instructions, and then suggested that we abandon our wait at the camp because it was most unlikely that the pair would return there. However, he invited me, Nicholas and Professor Carpenter to call at his office the following afternoon to catch up on developments.

Carpenter declined after checking that his presence wasn't essential, because his airline had promised him a flight earlier in the day, but Nicholas and I accepted with alacrity. We weren't going to abandon the business at this late stage, after all the effort we'd put into it.

We delivered Carpenter to the airport next morning, and after lunch in Nairobi we went round to Kambatini's office. Where we discovered that things had indeed been happening.

The police had raided Ruiru Highland Estates the previous evening. They could find no trace of the policeman who was supposed to have infiltrated the staff, but they found sawn-up sections of ivory in a workshop, and two sealed coffee chests each containing a layer of ivory at the bottom. Joyce and Dennis Smythe had been arrested, along with an African foreman.

There was now a nationwide alert for police and game park officials to watch for Pendleton and Motokwe, and to detain them for questioning. No trace had yet been found of Pendleton, but Motokwe had been seen driving a Huntsman Safari Land Rover along the road from Migori to Kisii, north-west of Masai Mara near Lake Victoria.

A road-block had been set up near Kisii, where the road divided to go to Kisumu and to Kericho, and Motokwe had attempted to circumvent this by detouring at speed through the bush. He had just about succeeded when his vehicle hit a deep pothole and lurched into a tree. He was thrown into the steering wheel and windscreen, and was severely injured and not expected to live. In the hospital he kept moaning 'I left him alone', which made no sense to anyone.

We stayed some days more in Kenya, and we drove around to a number of sites where Pendleton might have been found. It seemed likely that Motokwe had abandoned

Pendleton somewhere, possibly where he would have had trouble getting away – otherwise why would Motokwe have made the comment? However, none of us found the slightest trace, and Motokwe had died by that time so we couldn't ask him anything further.

We found this an unsatisfying end to our mission. If we'd been in a detective story there would have been a neat conclusion, but no such luck. Eventually we had to return to England to prepare for the new academic year, and the only further thing we can add is that a bit later we received a letter from Peter Marston. Apparently Monika had bumped into Ezekiel in Nairobi, and he'd reported that there'd been absolutely no further sighting or sign of Charles Pendleton and the police were now sure that he must have died, somehow and somewhere.

The one consolation in the whole sorry affair was that that particular ivory poaching operation had been well and truly demolished – a tiny win for the elephants. And to that extent Fergus Campbell had not died in vain, even if as far as we were concerned his death had not been properly avenged.

EPILOGUE

A few days after Pendleton had met the *siafu*, the sun set with a vivid carmine glow behind the western slopes of Masai Mara. A large elephant stood on one of the ridges, its long, straight tusks silhouetted against the crimson backdrop.

It raised its trunk, and trumpeted a call that reverberated over the hills and through the valleys, striking awe and fear into all that heard it.

And it slowly continued its walk, back to the great expanse of the plains of Serengeti....

AUTHOR'S NOTE

This story is set in 1985, when South Africa lived under apartheid with a mainly Afrikaner government. My wife Pam and I lived there from 1976-1979, working at Wits University in Johannesburg and a game reserve in the northern Transvaal (as it was called at the time).

Nicholas's thoughts on the contradictions of South Africa and its people are very much what my own were at the time. It was a fascinating experience, but the officially enforced discrimination of apartheid was ugly, at times violent, and often very petty. Our exposure to the wonderful wildlife of Africa made up for at least some of the meanness of the human population. Though like Carina, there were also some brave and principled people who stood up for justice and fairness.

ACKNOWLEDGMENTS

An invaluable reference for the topography, mammals and birds of Kenya's national parks and reserves was "A Field Guide to the National Parks of East Africa" by John G. Williams, illustrated by Rena Fennessey and published by Collins, London, in 1967.

I am enormously grateful to my wife Pam, who was my inspiration as we travelled to the various locations mentioned here, and then put up with my hours at the computer as I drafted the book.

All characters in the book are entirely fictitious, except for Chegi who was as good a camp cook for us as Marion and Nicholas had found him.